D0051979

macarons at
midnight

Suzanne Nelson

SCHOLASTIC INC.

For Aviva and Isaac, with love.

If you purchased this book without a cover, you should be aware that this book is stolen property. It was reported as "unsold and destroyed" to the publisher, and neither the author nor the publisher has received any payment for this "stripped book."

Copyright © 2015 by Suzanne Nelson

All rights reserved. Published by Scholastic Inc., *Publishers since 1920.* SCHOLASTIC and associated logos are trademarks and/or registered trademarks of Scholastic Inc.

The publisher does not have any control over and does not assume any responsibility for author or third-party websites or their content.

No part of this publication may be reproduced, stored in a retrieval system, or transmitted in any form or by any means, electronic, mechanical, photocopying, recording, or otherwise, without written permission of the publisher. For information regarding permission, write to Scholastic Inc., Attention: Permissions Department, 557 Broadway, New York, NY 10012.

This book is a work of fiction. Names, characters, places, and incidents are either the product of the author's imagination or are used fictitiously, and any resemblance to actual persons, living or dead, business establishments, events, or locales is entirely coincidental.

ISBN 978-0-545-88425-9

10 9 8 7 6 5 4 3 2 1   16 17 18 19 20

Printed in the U.S.A.   40
First printing 2016

k design by Jennifer Rinaldi

Chapter One

I knew my Valentine's Day was doomed when I glanced into the mirror and an amphibian monstrosity stared back at me. My outfit could've been a ballet costume from Cirque de Horriblé, with lime-green crinoline petals making up the sweeping, ankle-length skirt, and green and pink sequins glittering all over the leotard-like bodice. And I was going to a party in it? My social life in Whitman would never recover. I sagged against the bathroom door, then jumped when someone knocked on it.

"Elise, if you don't hurry up, we're going to be late." The voice was high, nasally, and *annoying*. Destry. I'd only been living with my stepsister for a week, but I could already tell by her tone when she was getting irritated, or impatient, or both. "Lise, *come on!*" Definitely both.

I sighed, then opened the door onto a hallway of expectant faces.

My dad took my hands, leading me out of the bathroom, and looked from me to Destry and back again. *"Lindo maravilhoso!"* he exclaimed. "Beautiful, marvelous! Would you look at my two *anjinhos!*"

My dad is from Brazil, so I'm used to him sprinkling Portuguese words in here and there. But he's never said *"anjinhos"*—plural—before. My stomach lurched. Since when did Dad call Destry his "little angel?" That was *my* nickname . . . not hers.

"Aaaaah, Lise." My stepmom, Gail, smiled from over the top of her ballooning baby belly. "You're so colorful . . . and cute!"

I smiled politely, but who was she kidding? She'd only tossed the *cute* in there as an afterthought to make up for *colorful*. Words like *colorful* and *interesting* were what people used when all flattering adjectives failed.

"That's such an interesting mask," Gail added. *Bingo*. She l̶ ̶ed forward for a closer look. "Your dad told me you made it

I nodded. My mask was a glittered green lily pad adorned with a pink flower and tiny gold frog. It was the only part of my garish outfit I actually liked.

"She's going as a frog," Destry quipped, giggling. "She already *sounds* like one."

"I'm getting over a cough," I muttered. No way was I going to admit that she was right. I'd been hoarse for the last week. "And I'm a frog *princess*," I corrected, stiffening.

"Of course! Very clever!" Gail tilted her head. "Destry . . . isn't that the costume from your seventh-grade *Nutcracker* ballet?"

Destry nodded, smiling. "Lise didn't have a costume and it's a masquerade party." She smoothed her own flawless white maxi dress, then adjusted her sparkling swan mask. It set off her platinum hair and fair skin beautifully. "It was the only thing I had that fit her," she added casually. "I'm taller than she is."

I stared at Destry, knowing that wasn't exactly true. There had been a gorgeous teal sheath dress in her closet that was just my size. When I'd suggested adding a feathered headband to make it into a peacock costume, Destry had blown off the idea.

"Oh no," she'd said. "That's the dress I wore to homecoming. It's special. I was crowned freshman princess in the homecoming court. Besides, this color would completely wash you out," she'd scoffed.

"Lise, wasn't that nice of Destry to loan you something?" Dad urged. "And to offer to take you along to the party?"

"Um . . . sure," I mumbled, my cheeks flushing. "Thanks, Destry." It was what he and Gail expected me to say. Last night, I'd overheard Dad and Gail telling Destry she *had* to bring me along.

"Lise doesn't know anyone here yet," Dad had whispered while I'd eavesdropped from the kitchen. "It would be a wonderful way to make her feel welcome."

"But she's a year younger than I am!" Destry had complained. "Freshmen don't hang out with eighth graders."

"At this party they do," Gail had said firmly. "I already spoke to Becca's mom about it. She said Becca's brother, Kyan, and some other eighth graders will be there. So you'll take Lise with you, or you won't go at all."

"Fine," Destry had snapped.

Today, though, I sensed Destry's growing grudge like an encroaching glacier. Of course, she was smooth enough to hide it from Dad and Gail. She smiled with those round blue doe eyes. "I'm glad you're coming along," she said to me. "It'll be fun."

"Well, just look at the two of you," Gail said, beaming and patting her belly, "already hanging out together. Swapping clothes. I knew it was a good idea for you to share a room."

I stared at the floor, not wanting my face to give me away. The fact was I hated sharing a room with Destry. She had a wardrobe to rival the Princess of Wales that constantly spilled over onto the floor and my bed. Plus, she had decorated the room to look like one enormous purple feather duster. When I'd tried to hang up my poster of "The Greatest Newspaper Headlines of All Time," Destry had said, "I'm not so sure that goes with our décor, are you?" Not wanting to pick a fight, I'd stuck the poster under my bed. Nothing about the room felt like me. Each time I set foot in it, I was trespassing on Destry's territory.

Dad held up his camera. "Okay, who's ready for a Kodak moment?"

"Dad, please. No pictures," I moaned. "We're already late." I definitely did not want my hideous outfit immortalized in the annals of the Santos family history.

"Lise is right," Destry said as a horn honked from the driveway. "That's Mrs. Michaels and Heidi now. We've got to go." She headed for the front door.

"All right," Dad said, making a show of putting down the camera in exasperation. He kissed me on the forehead. "Have fun. I'll see you in a few hours!"

Fun. My insides quaked nervously. Fun would be a long shot, but I promised myself to give it a try.

"Sorry we're late," Destry said to her equally glamorous friend Heidi as we climbed into the minivan. "Lise took forever to get ready."

I gaped at her. "You were in the bathroom for two hours before you let me have it for fifteen minutes!"

Destry shrugged. "You didn't need as much time. I had to straighten my hair, do my makeup. You never bother with any of that."

Heat swept my cheeks. Sure, I usually stuck with a more au naturel look. But tonight I'd actually brushed on some light mascara and lip gloss, and tucked my mane of thick espresso-colored hair into a knot. It was the best I could do with so little time, but apparently it hadn't done much at all.

I sank back, wishing I'd just opted to stay home tonight. I'd been in the small town of Whitman, Massachusetts, for a week, but it seemed like an eternity since I'd said good-bye to the cozy fifth floor walk-up I lived in with Mom and Bill in Boston.

My life had been going along perfectly. I was a mostly A student, editor-in-chief of the school paper, and I had a close-knit circle of friends I'd grown up with in the city. I'd even been glad when Mom married Bill a few months ago. I liked him, he loved Mom, and I loved seeing her so happy. It had been working out great . . . until Bill took a six-month work assignment in Switzerland, and Mom decided to go with him.

"It'll be fine," Mom had told me as I tried not to cry. "Your dad's been wanting to spend more time with you anyway. You can live with him this spring, finish out the school year, and then visit us in Switzerland for the summer."

Part of me had wanted to move to Switzerland with Mom and Bill. I'd always lived with Mom, and I barely knew Dad's new family. Before he remarried, he used to come into Boston every other weekend to see me, and during baseball season, we'd gone to almost every Red Sox game together. But since he married Gail, I hadn't seen as much of him. He'd invited me to Whitman over and over again, but I'd only visited a few times, feeling awkward around Gail and Destry. Still, though, the practical part of me argued to move in with Dad. Next year, I'd be starting high school. That was huge. But it meant I had to finish up eighth grade first, and it made sense for me to stay in the US to do it.

So here I was, in Whitman, dressed like a tulle-covered tadpole, being dragged to a Valentine's party, missing Boston more with each passing second.

"Here's the deal," Destry said when we arrived and climbed out of the van. "I'll introduce you around, but I'm not going to babysit you. I want to have fun with my friends tonight. Got it?"

"No problem," I said, trying to make my voice as cool and casual as possible. I climbed out of the van, gazing at Becca's lit-up house. A heart garland hung on the door. My own heart tossed uneasily in my chest. I hated parties; I hated small talk; I hated meeting new people. This was going to be a disaster.

I flattened myself against the heart-festooned wall of the living room, feeling invisible. True to her word, Destry had introduced me to some people, and then disappeared. There were other eighth graders at the party, but apparently Becca's brother, Kyan, was hiding in his room (I was jealous), and the other kids who were my age didn't seem interested in becoming my BFF.

Now, I watched as an eighth-grade girl named Vivika (Viv for short) stood in the center of the crowd, beautiful and model-tall in her Cinderella-esque gown.

"I can't believe you're doing a photo shoot for *Tween Glam* next week," one of the other girls was saying to Viv. (So she *was* a model. I'd nailed it.) "I sooo want your life. You probably get to meet such cool people."

Viv nodded, but the tiniest flutter of frustration crossed her face. "It's okay," she said, with less certainty than I'd expected. Could a reluctant model actually exist? "But I have to make up all the schoolwork I miss, and most of the time I'm actually just waiting around . . ." Her voice died as the girls looked at her in disappointment, and I guessed they'd probably hoped to hear some story about a celeb sighting instead. Then Viv's face brightened. "But I *do* get to keep the clothes! There's this dress that'll be perfect to wear to winter formal. Trent will love it."

Immediately, the girls erupted in twitters of excitement, and Viv's smile widened as she reclaimed her audience with a description of the dress. I thought about contributing a *cool* or a *wow* to get my foot in the conversational door, but just as I opened my mouth, Viv and her followers disappeared into the kitchen. I sagged against the wall, relieved that they were gone but also frustrated that I'd missed yet another chance to be social.

I scanned the room for Destry but didn't see her among the pink and red balloons and streamers. I knew Dad was coming to pick us up at eleven—it was nine-fifteen, and I didn't know how I could survive almost two more hours. I headed for a chair in the corner, weaving through the maze of masqueraders.

As I sat, I studied the room, and instantly saw a half a dozen headlines in front of me. My best friend from Boston, Simone, always joked that I couldn't turn off my journalist brain, and maybe it was true. Right now, the model-girl Viv seemed to be having a heated argument with the boy I could only assume was her boyfriend, Trent. Destry's BFF, Becca, was busy flirting with some boy dressed as Zorro. From the looks of things, there were at least two break ups happening, three crushes starting (CUPID'S ITCHY TRIGGER FINGER), plus a chocolate-eating contest (TOP TEN WAYS TO EAT YOUR HEART OUT THIS VALENTINE'S DAY!) at the snack table. I pulled my cell phone out of my clutch and texted Simone.

Me: Breakings news. LISE SANTOS HEADS FOR SOCIAL SUICIDE.

Simone: LOL. Quit headlining. Ur not trying hard enuf.

Me: EZ 4 u 2 say. Ur eating ice cream & watching vampire romance right now.

Simone: It's chocolate & zombies. Miss u.

Me: U 2

Suddenly, I heard the word *frog* float through the room, and I glanced up from my cell.

"I feel sort of bad for her, being Destry's Step and all," Viv was saying, not two feet from where I sat. Her back was turned to me, and I guessed she didn't have a clue I was within earshot. "She'll never get out from under Destry's shadow.

11

Especially dressed like that, poor thing. That tutu is the color of . . . of pond scum!" Laughter erupted around Viv, and even though I couldn't see her face, I was sure she had to be reveling in it.

I stared at her back. So now I didn't even have a name besides Destry's Step?! I leapt up, prepared to defend myself even if it meant making a scene in front of a room full of strangers. But the front of my skirt caught on something, and I heard a loud rip. I glanced down in time to see Viv slide her foot out from on top of my hem. Several of the crinoline petals on Destry's dress were torn and dragging along the floor.

"Oh no," I moaned, lifting the skirt to assess the damage. Destry was going to freak when she saw it. "It's ripped," I said helplessly, glancing at Viv.

Viv gasped, her cheeks blushing bright pink, and a flicker of dismay crossed her perfect features. "Oh . . . I'm . . . I didn't see you there." For a split second, she looked ready to apologize. But then Trent snickered from where he was standing a few feet away.

"Oblivious as always, Viv," he said. "All beauty, no brains."

Viv's blush deepened as she frowned at Trent, her lip trembling slightly. Then she straightened, glancing back at me. "It's your fault," she said matter-of-factly. "You weren't paying attention." Then she turned away.

"But . . . you . . . I mean . . ." The words died in my throat as my pulse roared, and suddenly, tears of humiliation were stinging my eyes.

I lifted my torn skirt and pushed past Viv, heading for the front door. I couldn't stay in this house a second longer. I didn't care what Destry did or didn't do. I was getting out of here.

I grabbed my jacket from the coat hanger and threw open the door, stumbling into the icy night air. I'd written a lot of articles for my school paper back home about the worst Valentine's Days ever, but there was no doubt about it. This one took the cake.

Chapter Two

I walked blindly in the crisp wintry silence, thankful that the darkness and my mask could hide my quivering lip and tear-filled eyes. That was one benefit to a New England country town. No streetlights or skyscrapers to put your face in the spotlight.

I had no idea where I was, or how to get home. Whitman was small, though, so I figured I'd recognize something. Sure enough, a few minutes later, I saw a golden glow up ahead, and turning the corner, found myself on Main Street. It was only two blocks long, with antique gas lights on either side of its cobblestone street, and every shop was dark. Except one: a store with a delicate wrought-iron gate and twinkling white lights draped over an awning that read, SWOONFUL OF SUGAR.

The windows glowed cozily with candlelight, and cious smell of butter and vanilla wafted out from the door as a customer walked inside. It looked so inviting, and the smell was so enticing, I stepped closer. When I did, an elderly woman appeared from under the awning. She had silver hair swept back in an elegant bun, and wore small pearl earrings, a sleek turtle-neck, and slacks that accentuated her slenderness. Looking at her standing before the twinkling storefront, I felt as if I was on some charming Parisian avenue.

"Bienvenue! Welcome!" she beckoned in a thick French accent, gently taking my hand. "I am Madame Leroux. And *this* is my patisserie." Her face shone with an air of wisdom and grace, and it was so kindly that I had the illogical urge to hug her. I settled on returning her smile instead. "You must come in!"

"I . . . I'm not sure—" I started, but she tsk-tsked at my protest.

"Nonsense. We are having a taste test inside to decide on our menu tonight for our grand opening next month." She led me through the door into a mustard-yellow room overflowing with laughing, chatting people, and even more sugary aromas.

A glass counter stretched the length of one wall. Inside was a pastel rainbow of the most beautiful, delicate pastries I'd ever seen.

"Have a seat," Madame Leroux told me as she bustled off.

I sighed, feeling my anxiousness easing in the patisserie's welcoming warmth. Every seat was taken except one across from a raven-haired boy bent intently over a sketchbook. He looked to be about my age, maybe a year older. His charcoal-smudged hand moved in quick, sure strokes across the page, and I could see he was sketching a tree with sweeping branches.

"Excuse me," I asked, stepping toward him. "Do you mind if I sit here?"

He was so focused on his work that he didn't seem to hear me, but when I asked a second time, his head whipped up, and my breath caught. His eyes were the most amazing color I'd ever seen—pecan shot through with green flecks—thoughtful with a hint of brooding on the side. Dark curls framed his angular, olive face, making those green flecks look like bright seedlings sprouting in a desert. And when he smiled . . . *oh, man.*

"Wow," he said, his eyes sparkling as he took in my outfit. "Did I miss Halloween?"

"Nope. The worst party of the century." I was glad my red-hot cheeks were hidden by my mask. I took off my jacket, then tried to squeeze between his table and the next to get to my chair but managed to spray him with a flurry of green petals from my costume. "Sorry." I finally sat down with an exasperated huff. "I know . . . I look ridiculous."

"No," he said quickly. "You look . . . pretty. For a frog."

I blushed again. "Frog *princess*," I corrected, feigning irritation.

He placed his hand over his heart and bowed slightly. "Forgive me . . . Your Sliminess. I mean, Your Highness."

I couldn't help but laugh as Madame Leroux appeared. "*Excusez-moi, mes petites*," she said, placing a plate with two heart-shaped, flaky pastries in between us. "These are *palmiers*. Please taste and then rate on your taste-testing tally sheet. I'll bring out a new pastry every few minutes." She smiled, her gaze batting back and forth between us with delight. "*Bon appetit!*"

We each reached for one. "This looks delicious," I said. "Flies can get *pretty* old, let me tell you."

The boy laughed, then held his *palmier* up. "Cheers!" he said amicably, tapping his pastry to mine.

I took a bite and my mouth instantly filled with zesty orange and butter flavors.

"Mmm. At least four out of five stars." I checked off the box on my tasting sheet.

"Pretty good." The boy took another bite, then looked at me quizzically. "Wouldn't it be easier to eat without the mask?"

I nodded and reached to take it off, then hesitated, remembering I was sitting across from the cutest guy I'd ever seen outside of the movies. What if I botched this the way I'd botched the party? What if I took the mask off, and he saw what I saw every time I looked in the mirror? A nothing-special sort of face that was easy to forget, and even easier not to notice in the first place? Brains had always been my strong point, not beauty, so maybe they'd work in my favor now.

I smiled as my hand dropped to the table. "Actually, I'm going incognito tonight," I said. "I prefer to remain an international frog of mystery."

He studied me, his face suddenly more serious. "That must have been one traumatic party."

I popped the rest of the *palmier* into my mouth. "You have no idea."

"Try me," he said.

He said it teasingly, but his face looked completely sincere. Madame Leroux slid another plate onto our table, this one with mini layered strawberries and cream cakes she called *fraisiers*. Suddenly, inexplicably, I wanted more than anything to pour my heart out to this total stranger.

"Well," I said as I nibbled my scrumptious *fraisier*, "the curse started when my possibly evil stepsister forced me to commit a fashion felony . . ."

The words blew out of me in a storm of venting. I was careful not to mention any names, though, especially Destry's. I couldn't stand the thought of this adorable guy labeling me "Destry's Step" along with everyone else. This town was so small, the high school and middle school shared the same campus.

By the time we were on a plate of *religieuses*, an éclair-style pastry topped with a ganache button, I'd told the boy all the gory details of my party fiasco.

"You're right," he said when I finished. "Worst party of the century." He pushed his *religieuse* toward me. "Here, have mine. Chocolate will ease the pain."

"Thanks." I shook my head. "I just keep thinking that it

would've been better if I'd stayed home tonight. Then I wouldn't have had to pretend to be someone I'm not."

He tilted his head. "Who were you pretending to be?"

I shrugged. "Someone . . . better at parties. Better at meeting new people. Someone who's *not* wallpaper."

"I don't know . . . You're pretty chatty for wallpaper." He grinned.

I giggled. "It's like when I'm in a roomful of people, I can never find anything to say. But when I'm comfortable and talking about stuff I believe in, I can't shut up." I blushed into my hands. "And I'm not making any sense, am I? So now, I really *am* going to shut up."

"I hope not," he said. "And I understand. I can be pretty quiet, too, except if I'm talking about things I'm passionate about."

"So, is one of your passions art?" I asked, nodding to his sketchbook. "I saw you sketching when I first came in." Then I added teasingly, "You were awfully serious."

"I was?" His eyebrows lifted in surprise, and an adorable apricot blush colored his cheeks. "Sometimes I get so involved in it, I forget where I am." He smiled sheepishly, making my heart flutter.

"Can I see?" I blurted, then silently scolded myself for being so pushy. "I mean," I backtracked, "only if you want to."

He hesitated for an excruciating second, but then he nodded, handing me his sketchbook. "Most of them are really rough," he said.

I opened the sketchbook and caught my breath. The first page was a drawing of a woman on a bike. Pastel lines of teal and pink streamed out behind her, mimicking the wind, while yellow starbursts popped up from the bike's spinning tires. The next was of a dog running with green grass shooting up in clumps from his trail of paw prints. They were so unique. They weren't just good, they were . . .

"Incredible," I said, just as a loose paper fluttered out from the sketchbook. I caught it right before it hit the floor, then gasped. "It's Boston Harbor," I breathed.

There were the boats with vanilla sails gracefully skimming the water; skyscrapers gleaming gold in the sun. It was part photograph, part painting, with brushstrokes of cobalt dabbing the water and sunflower yellow streaking up from the buildings.

"This . . . this one's my favorite," I said quietly, feeling a sharp pang of homesickness. "It's everything I love about Boston."

"Then you can keep it," he said. "You're the only person I've ever shown it to."

"Are you kidding?" I asked, staring at him. "What are you afraid of?" I cringed at his widening eyes, realizing I was shifting into reporter mode, asking personal questions. But his art was crazy good, and it didn't make sense that he'd hide it. "I mean . . . why?" I asked, gentler this time.

A line creased his forehead. "Because my art kind of . . . complicates my life. So I keep it to myself."

I wanted to know more, but the heaviness in his face made me drop it. Whatever the problem was, he didn't want to spill it. "Well . . . thank you for sharing it with me," I said, hugging the painting. "But . . . you didn't sign it. You have to." I held it out to him. "Please?"

His fingers brushed mine as he took the picture, and I felt a current charge through me. His eyes locked on mine for a brief second before he pulled away, and I wondered if he'd felt it, too. He grabbed a Sharpie from his satchel and scribbled across the bottom of the picture, grinning. "There," he said. "Signed, sealed, delivered . . ."

I'm yours, my heart sang. I scolded it for getting way, *way* ahead of itself. This wasn't some silly rom-com.

"*C'est bon,* my *tourtereaux.* My lovebirds!" I snapped out of my thoughts as Madame Leroux bent over us, smiling.

"Oh n-no," I stammered. "We're not—I mean—" My cheeks blazed with embarrassment. When I chanced a look across the table, the boy was smiling, making me blush even more.

"You're the last ones here, and it's closing time!" Madame Leroux told us.

"What?" I glanced around in disbelief at the empty chairs and snuffed candles. "Oh," I said, crestfallen. I wasn't ready to say good-night. Not even close.

"One last treat before you go," she said, setting down a plate of pastel pink, green, and yellow sandwich-shaped cookies. They were so cute and colorful, with a delicious-looking icing center. "These are macarons." Madame Leroux placed one in my palm. "You share the first one . . . like this." She showed me how to carefully twist it apart.

"Cheers," I said, my voice lilting nervously as the boy and I clinked our halves together before eating them. The pink macaron was spongy and crunchy all at once, with the creamy center melting on my tongue in hints of raspberry and vanilla. It was perfect.

"There." Madame Leroux clasped both our hands in satisfaction. "Two halves connect two people, eh?" She winked.

Shakily, I stood up and walked with the boy to the door. "Sweet dreams for St. Valentine's," Madame Leroux called to us before she closed the door, leaving us standing outside under a bright, star-sprinkled sky.

My heart galloped as his eyes turned to mine. "That was fun," I said, to break the silence. "I'm lucky I found this place."

"I am, too." His voice was so soft, I wasn't sure I'd heard him right. "You know," he continued, "I didn't want to come here tonight."

"Really?" I asked in surprise. "Why? Who doesn't want to eat yummy pastries?"

He laughed. "The food wasn't the problem. I was standing in for a kid who backed out of an assignment at the last minute." He frowned. "I wanted to ditch the whole thing to spend the night sketching, but I didn't have the guts. I guess I'm sort of . . . too responsible for my own good." He sighed. A sweet, bashful smile spread across his face, making him look even cuter. "Anyway, what I'm trying to say is . . . tonight was totally worth it."

I nodded. "Yeah, the food was amazing."

He shook his head. "The food's not what made it worth it," he said quietly. My heart trilled as he stepped closer to me. "I'd like to see you again," he said.

"I'm sure you will," I blurted, sounding as nervous as I felt. "'Cause it's such a small town and . . . and . . ." My voice died. I couldn't breathe, let alone think straight. "I mean, I'd like that."

He stepped closer.

"So how does the fairy tale go?" he whispered, leaning toward me. "The Frog Princess only becomes human again after . . ."

A kiss, I thought deliriously as I closed my eyes. I held my breath, waiting for his soft lips to brush mine. *My first kiss . . .*

"*Espera aí!* Hold it right there!" a stern voice bellowed in my ear, and I jumped as a hand clamped down on my shoulder. My dad glared down at me. "What do you think you're doing?"

"Dad, I—"

"It's after midnight! I spent the last hour driving around town looking for you. I was about to call the police." He latched on to my arm, firmly tugging me down the sidewalk toward where his car was parked at the curb. He threw open the door of the car and growled, "Get in . . . now!"

"But, Dad . . ." I glanced back toward the awning of Swoonful of Sugar, where the potential boy of my dreams was standing in a state of confusion.

"Wait!" the boy called out to me as I got into Dad's car. "I don't even know who you are! What's your name?"

I tried to pop my head out of the car. "It's—"

Clunk! The door slammed shut, and a second later, Dad peeled away like a NASCAR driver with a serious case of road rage. All I could do was helplessly stare through the rear window as my first-ever Valentine disappeared from sight.

Chapter Three

"Elise Anna Santos, what were you *thinking*?" Dad yelled as we sped through the streets. "How could you leave the party without telling anyone? Why didn't you call us? What possessed you to go traipsing around Whitman in the middle of the night? And who was that boy you were talking to?"

"Just a friend," I lied. I grimaced. I'd just lost my chance at a first kiss with the sweetest guy I'd ever met. I had no idea what his name was or if I'd ever see him again. But I tried to focus on apologizing to Dad.

"Dad, I said I was sorry a hundred times already," I tried. "I didn't mean to worry you. The party just . . . wasn't for me."

We pulled into the driveway, and Dad turned off the ignition.

"Inside," he said gruffly, getting out of the car. "Now. You owe Destry an apology."

I stared after him. He *couldn't* be serious. I skulked through the door and into the kitchen, where Destry was bent over her cell phone, her thumbs flying over the screen, probably texting the entire Whitman population that I was single-handedly destroying her life.

"*Now* you show up," she snapped when she saw me. "Becca's mom freaked when we couldn't find you. The party ended early, thanks to you. And I didn't even get to dance with Jake!"

I inhaled sharply. "I just took a walk to kill some time. I didn't realize how long I was gone . . ."

Destry gave my dad a helpless look. "I really wanted to include her tonight," she said, acting as if I wasn't even in the room anymore. "I thought it would give us a chance to get to know each other better. But I can't help her if she doesn't at least try to make friends."

Then she glanced in my direction, and I shuddered as her eyes landed on the dragging, ripped hem of my dress.

"My *Nutcracker* costume!" she shrieked. "Look what you did to it. It's ruined!"

"It was an accident," I said helplessly. "Viv stepped on it, and—"

"That costume means a lot to me." Destry sniffed. "I loaned it to you because I thought you'd be careful with it."

"I *was* careful!" I said, my voice rising to match hers. I threw up my hands. "But . . . but you're not even listening!"

Dad stepped between us, holding up a hand for silence. "All right, Lise, we're listening. What is it you'd like to say?"

Dad's eyes bored into me, silently imploring me to keep the peace. I heaved a breath. "I'm sorry about your dress," I said. "And I'm sorry about leaving the party. I messed up." I stared at the floor. "It won't happen again."

"Well . . . apology accepted," Destry said reluctantly. I had the feeling that she was disappointed I'd given up without more of a fight.

"And it *definitely* won't happen again," Dad said. "Because tomorrow you're going to spend the day cleaning the house as punishment."

What?!? my brain screamed. But through gritted teeth, I said, "Okay. Can I go to bed now?"

"*Sim, sim.* Yes. I'm tired, too." Dad glanced at Destry. "Destry, you know your mom's rule. Ten more minutes texting, and you're in bed. Understood?"

Destry's shoulders tensed, but she gave a clipped, "Fine."

I tiptoed upstairs, glad to have a few minutes to myself in the bedroom before Destry blew in. Frustration prickled under my skin. Up until a week ago, the time I'd had with Dad was so limited and special, he'd never had to scold me for much. We'd never had an argument before, and it made me feel oddly off-balance, like the ground was seesawing.

A knock on the door shook me out of my thoughts, and Dad called, "Can I come in?"

"Sure." Could I really say no when it wasn't my room to begin with?

"I wanted to say good night." Dad sat down tentatively on the edge of my bed, his thick, graying hair disheveled from where he'd been worrying it with his fingers. "You know, that's the first time I ever had to discipline you. I'm not sure I'm very good at it."

I gave a short laugh, and I felt a small crack in the tension between us. "No, no, if Mom were here, she'd applaud your punishment," I teased. "I *hate* cleaning. Especially bathrooms. Ugh."

Dad chuckled. "I remember your mother always hated that, too." He studied my face. "Do you miss her?"

I dug my toe into the carpet, not wanting to admit how badly. "A little."

"I know." Dad squeezed my hand. "This is a big change . . . for everyone." He smiled. "*Minha filha*, Gail and I are so excited to have you here with us." He kissed me lightly on the forehead and turned to the door. "Let's forget what happened tonight. We'll start fresh tomorrow."

"Okay," I said.

When he flipped off the light, I settled back against my pillow and closed my eyes, replaying my night at Swoonful in my head. There he was behind my eyelids . . . the boy with the blooming-desert eyes. I thought about how easily we'd fallen into talking, how I'd forgotten all the rules of flirting and getting-to-know-you conversations, and it hadn't even mattered. Connections like the one I'd felt tonight didn't happen every day. This was a gift from serendipity, and I wasn't going to waste it. He was the best thing that had happened to me since I moved to Whitman, and I wasn't going to let him get away.

"Hey, Princess!"

My heart catapulted as I jerked to a stop beside a row of lockers. It was *him*. I grinned and spun around, searching the throngs of students for the face that had become a permanent fixture in my brain.

But it was only some guy from Becca's party, calling to Viv, who was chatting with some girls across the hall. Disappointment flooded through me. Oh . . . right. Viv *had* been Cinderella at the party, after all. I swiftly turned away before she saw me.

The third period bell rang. I hurried through the hallways, relieved when I found my Biology classroom relatively quickly. It was my first day of school, and I'd gotten lost going to first and second period.

I walked through the door to see a dozen kids huddled in the corner, staring at something on the floor. The something, I realized with a start, was a very large, very alive tarantula.

"Can't we just squash it already?" one girl squeaked.

"No way!" scolded a voice, and a tall, gangly boy stepped out of the huddle, glaring at her from behind his glasses. "Herb is

Mr. Vern's pet. How would you like it if someone tried to exterminate your dog?" When the boy scooped the tarantula into his hand, everyone took a step back. "Spiders have feelings, too, you know," he added as he deposited Herb safely back into his terrarium.

There was a collective sigh of relief when the lid was secured, and within seconds, the other kids dispersed into smaller, chit-chatting groups, already seeming to forget Herb and his rescuer.

"That was brave," I offered, since no one else had even bothered with a "thank you."

"Not really," the boy said, "Herb's completely harmless. But thanks, anyway." His hazel eyes scrutinized me. "Hey . . . you're Lise Santos, right?"

I nodded. "How'd you know?"

"Mr. Vern mentioned you'd be in our class. And Becca told me all about you. I'm Kyan Slade, Becca's brother." He paused. "So what happened with the party? My mom went all Amber Alert when you went missing."

"Yeah, I heard." I sighed, feeling bad about my disappearing act. "Parties aren't really my thing, so I ended up going to a taste test at Swoonful of Sugar. It was actually amazing. But I'm sorry I caused so much drama."

"Hey, I don't blame you for ditching the party." Kyan grinned. "I spent the night bonding with my emperor scorpion, Napoleon. I'm way too much in the nerd camp for my sister's parties." He motioned to Herb the Tarantula. "I'm sort of a freak for bugs. So . . . how's your first day going?"

"Okay," I started, then sighed. "Actually, lousy. I feel like everybody looks *at* Destry and looks *through* me." When Dad had dropped us off that morning, a literal swarm of kids flocked to Destry, surrounding her within seconds and leaving me standing on the outskirts, alone. "Every kid in this school has some story they're dying to tell me about her. Teachers, too!" I shook my head. "I was late to first period English because the school secretary was telling me how in last year's *Swan Lake*, Destry was the most graceful dancer she'd ever seen."

Kyan nodded sympathetically. "It's tough being the socially challenged sibling of an A-lister. Believe me, *I* know. It's why most of my friends have six legs." He looked only mildly bothered by this, and I wondered if he was the sort of person who wasn't totally affected by status. My friends in Boston were like that. "The Independents," we called ourselves. It would be so nice to have that in a friend here, too. "You just have to find your niche, that's all."

"I guess," I said. I wasn't ready to admit to the other reason why I was having such a bad day: the fact that I'd been hoping to see the boy I'd met Saturday night. But hadn't . . .

"Let's see your schedule," Kyan said now. "Lunch break is after this, and I can show you where your other classrooms are." A sheepish look crossed his face. "I usually eat in the Science Club room, you know, to study the specimens and stuff. But I can eat in the caf with you today, give you the rundown of 'who's who,' that sort of thing. I mean . . . if you want."

I smiled. *All you need is one friend there,* Simone had told me right before I left Boston. *Just one, and you'll be fine.*

"That would be great," I told Kyan. "Thanks."

"You'll love Mr. Vern," Kyan whispered as class started. "And if you like Herb, wait until you see Stan. He's the foot-long millipede behind Mr. Vern's desk."

"Cool," I said, wondering what the odds were of the foot-long millipede escaping, too. Then again, it looked as though I might have found my "one" friend in Whitman, and if bugs were his thing, well, then . . . bring on the antennae.

"Well, here's something that Whitman and Boston have in common." I pushed the meat loaf around on my tray. "Disgusting hot lunch."

"See?" Kyan said jovially, elbowing me. "It's already starting to feel like home, right?" He unpacked a delicious-looking turkey sandwich from his lunch sack. "First rule for surviving WMS. Never ever buy lunch on Mystery Meat Mondays." He lifted his sandwich, but it froze halfway between the table and his mouth.

"Kyan?" I said, peering at his goggling eyes. "What's the matter?"

I followed the path of his stare to see Viv walking toward us with the same group of girls I'd seen her with this morning. I felt a fresh wave of irritation and sat up straighter, thinking that if I couldn't avoid her, this time I'd be brave enough to give her a real piece of my mind.

I opened my mouth, but before I could utter a sound, Viv was sliding onto the bench beside me.

"Thank goodness I found you, Lise." She said it with such earnestness that I could only stare, speechless. "I've been looking for you all morning."

Wait . . . *what?*

In confusion, I looked from her to her group of friends, who were standing there, chattering among themselves about what to get for lunch. It didn't seem as if this was some sort of trap to mock me . . . so was she being sincere?

"I feel horrible about the way I treated you at the party," she went on worriedly, running a nervous hand through her caramel-colored hair. "I know I was totally rude, and that's not like me. But I was having the worst night *ever.*"

"Really?" I blurted, my curiosity finally giving me back my voice. This I *had* to hear.

She nodded, her glossed lips forming a perfect pout. "I got into this big fight with my boyfriend, Trent." She frowned, shaking her head. "*Ex*-boyfriend, I mean. He made me feel like such an idiot when I stepped on your dress, and I was so flustered . . . I just said everything wrong. Right after you left, we broke up."

"Yeah, and he didn't deserve you!" Kyan piped up, and Viv glanced at him. "I mean," he blustered, mumbling. "I thought he, um, should've treated you better. That's all."

Viv smiled, raising a surprised eyebrow in Kyan's direction. "Thanks."

He stared at her with unmistakable puppy-dog adoration, and suddenly I understood what was going on. A headline popped into my head: UNREQUITED LOVE LEAVES SPIDER-MAN HANGING.

Poor Spidey.

Kyan was opening and closing his mouth, trying to respond to Viv's thanks but failing. He finally gave me a panicked "Help me" look, and I came to the rescue, jumping in with, "That's . . . too bad. About your breakup. How long were you together?"

"Two weeks," Viv said with the same weightiness she might've used to say "two years."

"A record," a redheaded girl in the group snorted. "Viv goes through boys like ice cream. Trent was the Flavor of the Month."

"Come on, Mona. I'm not that bad," Viv said with a frown. But then as a blonde-haired boy breezed by the table, she laughed, giving a little shrug. "Okay, maybe I am. Check out Griffin. He's getting so tall . . ."

Mona rolled her eyes. "Here we go. Another insta-crush."

"What! Guys are like shoes, okay?" Viv said. "I have to keep trying them on until I find the perfect fit."

I laughed, but Mona yawned, as if the whole thing was boring her. "I'm going to get something to eat."

The other girls chimed in their agreement and headed for the lunch line. Viv called after them, "Be there in a sec!" Then she grinned at me. "Anyway, I'm *really* sorry about the other night. My mom is great at sewing. She used to make my pageant costumes when I was younger." She leaned toward me conspiratorially. "I *hated* my pageant dresses. They were so gaudy! But they never fell apart, even though I prayed that they would." She sighed. "I'm sure she could fix that tear in your dress."

"That would be amazing," I said. "Because it wasn't my dress. It was Destry's."

Viv gripped my arm, her eyes flying open. I expected her to give me another "Hail, Queen Destry" moment, but instead she surprised me with, "Omigod, I'm even sorrier now! Was she completely peeved?"

"Pretty much," I said, delighted that she wasn't jumping to Destry's defense. "But I got in even more trouble with my dad because I left the party . . ."

"I know," Viv said with a worried frown. "Where did you go?"

Before I knew it, I was filling in Viv and Kyan (who was still silent and staring at Viv in a love-sick haze) on my encounter with the mystery boy and the macarons. I figured, what did I have to lose? One of them might know who he was.

"That is *so* romantic." Viv smiled dreamily when I'd finished. "See? Why can't I find a guy like that? Someone nice, who looks at me and doesn't just see the cover of *Tween Glam* magazine."

"You were on the cover?" I asked.

"Twice," Kyan piped up. "June and November."

After he spoke, he turned red and commenced an Incredible Shrinking Snail act.

"So, your guy's an artist," Viv said, tapping her chin. "There's Liam, this guy in my English class. I heard he paints with his toes."

"No," I said. "My guy's name starts with *R*." The painting of Boston Harbor had been signed with a big *R*, followed by a series of squiggles that may as well have been Sanskrit.

"Why don't you check out the art room?" Kyan suggested. "You could take the painting he gave you to Mr. Diaz, the art teacher. He might recognize the signature."

I brightened. "That's a great idea! I'll bring in the painting tomorrow."

Viv's cell phone buzzed and she checked it, then squealed. "Mona texted me!" She nodded to where she was sitting a few tables over. "Griffin just sat down at our table. Gotta go." She stood up. "I'm glad we talked," she said. "Bring the dress into school, and I'll give it to my mom." She waved to us, then called over her shoulder. "I want a full report on Operation Mystery Boy tomorrow!"

"I think she really means it," I said after she walked away. "Hmm. She's nice. Not anything like I imagined."

"Yeah." Kyan stared after her longingly. "I've known her since preschool. We used to dig for worms together on the playground." He laughed a little. "That was way before her mom got her into pageants and modeling. Viv probably doesn't even remember."

"So . . ." I nudged Kyan with my elbow. "How long have you had a crush on her?"

"What? I don't! I mean, are you kidding?" He blew out a breath, his shoulders shaking with nervous laughter. "She's a *Morpho helena*, and I'm a grub." When I looked at him blankly, he added, "*Morpho helena*, the most beautiful butterfly on the planet?" He shook his head in disappointment, then added teasingly, "Man, if you're going to be my partner for Bio lab, you're going to have to do better than that."

I saluted him. "Hey, my grades are the only A-list I belong to. I'll make you proud."

The bell rang, and we tossed our trash and headed for our lockers. Kyan gave me his email and cell number so that I could call him if I needed help with my Bio homework, then pointed me in the direction of my Algebra classroom. "I'll see you later."

"Sure." I nodded. "Hey . . . Kyan?" He turned again. "Thanks for your help. You made my first day a lot easier."

"You're welcome." He grinned, then waved. "*Morpho helena*," he called as he walked away. "Look it up! It'll blow your mind."

I laughed, but as I turned down the long hallway, I felt some of my first-day jitters returning. Kyan had seen me through lunch, the most daunting task for any new student, but I'd be on my own for the last three periods of the day.

I found my Algebra classroom (whew!) and was just about to walk in when I caught sight of a flyer on the hall bulletin board.

THE *MINUTEMAN* SEEKS NEW STAFF REPORTER. POSITION AVAILABLE ASAP. EMAIL WRITING SAMPLE AND A COMPLETED APPLICATION TO MINUTEMAN@WHITMANMS.ORG.

My heart leapt excitedly. A position on the school paper! I'd certainly had plenty of experience in Boston. Kyan was right. I needed to find my niche, and this seemed like the perfect fit.

I quickly jotted down the website before heading into class, feeling a fresh wave of courage. If I did something familiar, maybe my new life here wouldn't feel so foreign. And maybe *I* wouldn't feel so out of place.

Two hours later, I didn't just feel out of place. I was *in* the wrong place. Or on the wrong bus anyway. When Hugh the bus driver dropped me back at school after finishing his circuit, the campus was deserted. The only car in the parking lot was Gail's, and as I walked toward it, I could see Destry's scowling face shooting death rays at me through the window.

"Oh, Lise, I'm so sorry," Gail said, casting a worried glance over her shoulder as I slid into the backseat. "I knew I should've picked you up today. I was afraid something like this would happen . . ."

"It's fine," I said quietly as the car moved out of the parking lot. "I got the bus number wrong or something." My face burned as I remembered the mortification I felt when the bus made its last stop, and the bus driver realized I wasn't getting off.

I'd only had to walk two blocks to my school in Boston. This bus thing was new, unchartered territory. Where was Kyan, my walking-talking school directory, when I needed him? Answer: on the *right* bus.

Destry harrumphed from the front seat. "Lise, there are only *three* middle school buses. *Three!* How could you have gotten on the wrong one?"

"Destry—" Gail started.

"No! Seriously!" She folded her arms and slumped down in the front seat. "I'm missing ballet because of *her*!"

"Sorry," I mumbled, wanting nothing more than this drive to be over so that I could get out of the car and out from under her glare. Why did it feel as if all I'd done since I'd arrived in Whitman was apologize to Destry?

In the rearview mirror, I could see the crease on Gail's forehead deepen, her mouth turn down slightly. Then, just as quickly, her smile returned. "You know, I'm glad this happened." Her voice was too high and a little too bright. "I've been trying to pick out paint colors for the nursery. Maybe you girls can help me decide."

Silence stretched out into the car as I waited for Destry to take Gail's cue. When she didn't, I said, "Sure." It didn't sound as convincing as I'd hoped, so I threw in a "We'd love to" for good measure. There was a barely audible scoff from Destry.

"That's a relief," Gail said. "We don't want your future sister or brother getting colicky over clashing colors."

As soon as the car pulled into the driveway, Destry was stomping up the front walk, her dance skirt fluttering behind her in the breeze. When I walked in behind Gail, the sweet vanilla scent of fresh-baked cake swept over me. I thought back to Swoonful of Sugar.

"Mmmm . . . what smells so good?" I asked.

Gail beamed, motioning me into the kitchen. "Boston Cream Pie. I baked one this afternoon, in honor of your first day of school."

"You did?" I said, not meaning to sound as disbelieving as I did. "It's my favorite."

Gail nodded. "Your dad told me. He used to take you for a slice at the Omni Parker House in Boston." She eyed the floor bashfully. "I doubt mine comes close, but I wanted to do something to say . . . welcome."

"Thank you," I said with a smile, touched that she'd gone to so much trouble for me. I searched the kitchen and found the pie sitting, mouth-watering and . . . half eaten, on the counter.

Gail blushed. "I already had a helping . . . or maybe three."

She glanced at me sheepishly, and then we both burst out laughing just as Destry blew into the kitchen, wearing sweats and a messy ponytail, as if to prove her misery at missing dance.

"So, are we looking at paints or what?" she asked impatiently.

"Oh! Yes!" Gail handed me a plate of pie as we sat down at the table in front of a thick color wheel of paint swatches.

"You could do purple," Destry suggested, and I tried not to roll my eyes. Of course she'd want purple.

"I actually want something gender neutral," Gail said. "I was thinking maybe . . . yellow? Or pastel green?"

"Those are nice," I offered, as Gail pointed out the swatches she'd had in mind, but Destry wrinkled her nose.

"Ick," she said. "Definitely not that awful puce."

Gail looked uncertain. "It's not *that* bad, Des," she said a little defensively.

"What about a soft teal?" I said. "Sort of oceany?" I held up a swatch, and Gail smiled.

"I don't like it," Destry said flatly, then looked at me. "And *you're* not the one who's going to be living with it anyway."

"Destry!" Gail's voice was sharper than I'd ever heard it before.

"Well, she *is* going back to her mom's at some point, isn't she?"

Silence settled over us. It was true enough, so why did it sting so badly when she said it?

Gail gave me a tremulous smile. "I hadn't even thought of that color, Lise," she said softly. "It's lovely."

Destry stood, grabbing her cell. "Look, if no one's going to listen to me, forget it. I'm going over to Becca's."

Gail sighed as the front door slammed, then turned back to me. "I'm sure she didn't mean that to come out so rudely."

"No, it's okay," I said quickly, standing up as the warm hopefulness I'd felt earlier dissolved. "I don't know much about decorating anyway. You should pick whichever color you like best. I have, um, some stuff to do."

"Oh, okay." Gail's face sagged.

Guilt nagged my stomach as I left the room. I didn't want to disappoint her, but Destry had a point. This wasn't my house, and once I went back to Mom's, I probably wouldn't see the new baby much, either. Maybe I shouldn't have a say in how the nursery was painted.

I went into the den and turned on the computer to check my email, desperately hoping there'd be something from my friends back in Boston. Sure enough, there were two emails from Simone, including a selfie video she'd taken singing "You . . . You will survive!" at the top of her lungs. I grinned. There were also emails from Nicole, Jenn, and my other friends, full of sweet "Miss Us" and "XOs." Reading through them made me smile. Whitman might not like me, but Boston loved me. It was still home.

I spent a few minutes on emails, and then pulled up the *MinuteMan*'s website and began filling out the job application. The sooner I found something here to keep me busy, the better.

I focused intently on my application, carefully recounting my experience as editor-in-chief and providing some of my favorite articles as writing samples. It was only after I emailed the application to the press that my heart sank. I realized I'd left Gail's Boston Cream Pie sitting, uneaten, on the table.

I hurried into the kitchen, but Gail was nowhere to be seen, and the pie was stashed in the fridge, covered in tinfoil. When I checked upstairs, Gail's bedroom door was closed. I started to knock, but my hand froze. Was that muffled crying I heard behind the door?

Oh, this was bad. I knew what headline I'd see scrawled across Dad's forehead at dinner tonight: DAD DISOWNS DAUGHTER FOR TRAUMATIZING EXPECTANT STEPMOM. Sometimes, it was painfully easy to read the writing on the wall.

Chapter Four

"Is that him?" Kyan pointed to a photo of a smiling black-haired boy. "Robert Staten?"

"No," I said dejectedly as I stirred my yogurt.

"Ack." Viv gritted her teeth.

"I'm telling you, his photo's not in here." I sighed. "Seriously, we've gone through it at least five times, start to finish."

We'd been flipping through the pages of Viv's yearbook since lunch started, without any luck. Scouring the yearbook had been her idea, after our other attempts to find "Romeo" (as Viv had nicknamed him after finding out his first name started with R) had failed. I'd taken Romeo's painting to the art room during lunch on Tuesday, but Mr. Diaz hadn't been able to give me any new leads.

"I wish I could say I knew who it was," he'd said. "This piece is one of a kind. But if one of my students experimented with mediums like this, believe me, I'd remember." As I was leaving, he called out, "If you find him, tell him I want his work in the school art show in March. No excuses!"

Every day while I waited for the bus (yes, I'd managed to find the right one after Monday's disaster), I searched the students' faces but never saw *him*. Now it was Friday, and a whole week had gone by since I'd last seen him. With each passing day I felt deeper disappointment and a growing fear that I'd missed my chance. What if he didn't go to my school at all? Worse, what if he didn't even live in Whitman?

Now, Kyan rubbed the top of his fuzzy cropped hair, a habit I'd noticed over the course of our week together. It usually meant he was about to say something he was afraid no one wanted to hear. It was one of the endearing traits about Kyan, who I'd begun thinking of as a semi-goofball surrogate brother. I'd glommed on to him as my school and town tour guide, but he didn't seem to mind. In fact, I suspected he may have been as much in need of a friend as I was. It was one of those Introverts Unite moments.

"Is it possible," he started hesitantly, "that you don't remember what he looked like? I mean, you said it was dark in the patisserie, and you were wearing your mask—"

"Ky-an." I drew out his name for frustration's sake. "I remember *exactly* what he looked like."

Viv gave him a playful slap on the arm, and Kyan blushed madly. "Of course she does. Nobody forgets the face of true love."

"Faces, in your case," I said teasingly.

"Watch it!" Viv said, elbowing me. Since Monday, Viv had seamlessly moved on from a flirtathon with Griffin to one with Ben *and* Holden, at the same time. One of them was taking her to the movies tonight, and the other tomorrow. Watching them argue over who would carry her books for her between classes was more entertaining than an episode of *The Bachelorette*.

Three days ago, I never would've risked a dig at one of the school's most beautiful and popular girls, but just like with Kyan, Viv and I were starting to reach a friendship comfort zone. Behind Viv's flawless model looks was a funny, spirited girl who orbited around the school's cliques without ever settling into any one for long. She was as comfortable eating lunch with Kyan and me as she was with Mona, Griffin, and their more glamorous crowd. She seemed so well liked that if she'd decided to run for student body president, she would've been a shoo-in. Of course, when I'd suggested that, she'd laughed airily.

"Me?" She rolled her eyes. "My mom would never let me. Not with the amount of school I have to miss for photo shoots." Still, though, she'd smiled at the idea.

Now, her brow crinkled as she tapped the cover of the yearbook, lost in thought. "I've got it!" she cried. "You can't find your guy because he's in the *high school*!" She propped her chin up on her elbow and grinned at me slyly. "Ooooh, you've snagged the heart of an older man!"

"I guess it's possible," I said. "But he didn't look that much older than us. He could be a freshman."

"*R, R, R . . .*" Viv mumbled, then she locked eyes with Kyan, and both their faces lit up.

"Raphael!" they cried simultaneously.

"Who?" I asked blankly.

"Raphael Moretti," Kyan said. "He's a freshman at the high school. He moved here halfway through eighth grade . . ."

"Which would explain why he's not in last year's yearbook," Viv said. "He missed school picture day."

"His name starts with *R*," Kyan continued, sounding more optimistic by the second, "he has dark hair, olive skin, and I think he won an award in the school art show last year!"

My heart lifted hopefully. "Sounds like it could be him."

"Yes!" cried Viv, high-fiving Kyan. "We've solved the mystery of the Romeo Romance." She nudged Kyan. "We make a great team."

"Yup," Kyan said, beaming deliriously. He was finally getting braver around Viv, talking more, breaking out of the snail shell. But he never stopped looking smitten around her, and Viv never seemed to pick up on it. "We can look for him after dismissal today."

Viv stood up to throw away her lunch trash. "I'll meet you at the flagpole." She clapped her hands gleefully. "There's no way I want to miss this reunion."

"We might miss the bus, though," Kyan said to me. "But I'll walk home with you after. Your street's on my way."

I nodded. "I'll text Gail to let her know, but I think that should be okay." Even though it was blustery cold outside, walking would be a nice change. It felt more natural to me than sitting on the stuffy bus anyway. Besides, it would be good to learn the way home, just in case I ever missed my bus again.

The bell rang, and we hurried to our lockers. I texted Gail while I walked, and as I did, my inbox pinged with a new email. I opened it and grinned. It was from the *MinuteMan Press*, requesting an interview with me on Monday after school. I quickly emailed back a confirmation and walked into Algebra with rising spirits.

Things were looking up. I had a legit chance at a job on the school paper, and within a few hours, I might finally come face-to-face with my Romeo.

"Here he comes!" Viv whisper-shrieked, jabbing her finger at the crowd of high schoolers spilling out of the doors. "He's the guy in the quilted green parka. See him?"

I scanned the sea of coats and hats, finally honing in on a forest green jacket. My heart clattered louder than my chattering teeth as my eyes traveled from his coat to his face. It had to be him. *Please let it be him.*

"It's not him," I said. My stomach buckled under the weight of my disappointment.

"Are you sure?" Kyan asked. "He's wearing a hat. Maybe you should go up to him . . ."

"I'm sure." His features weren't anything like I'd remembered, and his eyes were a bright blue. All wrong. "Raphael's not my Romeo."

Viv sighed, wrapping her coat tighter around herself. "Sorry, Lise."

"Thanks." I tucked my face further into my scarf to hide my wilting expression. "I guess that's it, then."

"No!" Kyan said, so forcefully that Viv and I both turned our heads to stare. "I mean, even if it's impossible, if you know it'll never happen, it doesn't matter. When you like someone that much . . ." His voice faded as he blushed. "When you like someone that much, a small part of you always keeps fighting, even when the rest of you gives up."

"Wow," Viv said appreciatively. "It sounds like you're talking from experience."

It did, but Kyan shrugged, staring at the ground. I wondered if he realized he'd given himself some sort of accidental pep talk about Viv.

"So what's next?" I asked. "I tried everything . . ."

"Maybe you should stop trying," Viv said, "and see if he finds you. Maybe he's looking for you just like you're looking for him."

She glanced toward the parking lot. "Oh, I have to run. My mom's here to pick me up, and I have to get ready. Tonight's the movies with Holden." She blushed, then added, "Sorry. I feel bad ditching you for a date . . ."

"Don't be," I said, making my voice brighter. "Just because I don't have my Romeo, doesn't mean you shouldn't have yours. I'm happy for you."

"Yeah, me too." Kyan's voice came out muffled. He'd pulled his mouth into his scarf and was studying the pavement intently.

"I want details later!" I said, knowing that was the good-friend thing to say, even though I wasn't much in the mood to hear Viv raving about her crush.

Viv waved as she headed for the parking lot. "I'll text you!"

Kyan and I turned to walk home, with him looking as morose as I felt.

"I can't believe Viv's going out with Holden," he mumbled, shaking his head. "I give her a week with him before it falls apart."

"Maybe not," I said, wanting to cling to *some* optimism about boys, no matter how small.

Kyan raised an eyebrow at me. "He's an even bigger jerk than Trent." He sighed. "I know Viv and I will never happen. But, just once, I'd like her to end up with a nice guy, you know? That's the worst part."

I nodded. I totally got that. Sometimes you wanted happiness for people you loved even when how they found it made *you* unhappy. I remembered feeling that way about my parents' divorce.

"You know what the worst part of today was for me?" I said. "Realizing that I'll never figure out who Romeo is. He's out there somewhere, but he isn't thinking about me. He's forgotten all about the Frog Princess."

And after what had just happened with Viv, poor Kyan didn't even have the heart to disagree.

"It's a mistake," Simone said, her voice tinny and garbled with bad cell reception.

"What?" I strained to hear her. "A mistake? So you *don't* think I should stop looking for him? I can't hear you!"

"It's FATE!" she hollered. I yanked my head away from my cell. "I *said*, 'If you stop looking for him and he still turns up, it's fate!'"

"Heard you loud and clear that time," I muttered.

"*Finally*," she grumbled. "All I'm saying is, don't turn a blind nose to the smell of destiny. Or . . . something like that. If it's meant to be, it will happen." There was a pause as static crackled the line. "Yeesh, where are you anyway, a tool shed? I heard rumors that those exist outside the city limits."

"Funny." I sighed. "No . . . I'm sitting on the floor in the upstairs bathroom. I can't talk in Destry's room. This is the only place I have any privacy."

"Really? In a two-story house? Do I need to take a train out there to kick somebody's butt?"

I laughed, not realizing until just then how much I missed my BFF's sarcastic sense of humor. It felt so good to hear it. "Not yet, but you're my in-case-of-emergency call button. I'll keep you posted." She laughed, and I smiled. "So . . . how are things back home?"

"Oh, the usual. Nicole's fighting with her 'rents and school is a complete drag." There was crunching over the line, and I imagined her munching caramel popcorn, her favorite. "Boston's just not the same without you."

"I'm not the same without it, either," I said, then jumped at a loud knock on the bathroom door.

"Come on, Lise!" It was the Voice of Chronic Irritation. "You've been in there for a half an hour," Destry whined.

"Gotta go, bye," I whispered into the phone, then to Destry, called, "Be out in a sec!"

"There better be hot water left," Destry snapped, blowing past me as I opened the door.

Brush it off, I told myself as I walked away. I'd decided that was going to be my new technique when dealing with Destry. The less I responded to her moodiness, the better. Maybe she was testing me, setting me up for situations where I'd get into trouble. Well, I wasn't going to let her sabotage me anymore. No way.

I straightened my shoulders, confident that I could beat Destry at her own game, grabbed my Red Sox hat from my bedpost, and went in search of Dad. He'd been working late at his law office most of this week, and I'd barely seen him except in passing in the hallway for a quick "good night" before bed.

He'd never mentioned anything about Gail being upset with me, much to my relief. But now I was starting to wonder if it wasn't work but disappointment with me that was making him distant.

I found him in the soon-to-be nursery, frowning as he bent over a partially built crib. Sweat beaded on his forehead as he twisted a screwdriver.

"Hey, Dad. How's it going?" I peered into the lopsided crib, which teetered precariously as Dad fiddled with its railing.

"*Muito mal.* Badly," he mumbled. "I don't remember *your* crib being this complicated." The screwdriver slipped and he lurched forward, then hissed through gritted teeth. "*Aff!* My back can't take much more of this." He sighed.

"So . . . how about a break?" I said brightly, seeing my perfect opportunity. "You remember what's on TV tonight, right?" He'd mentioned it when he'd first picked me up from Mom's two weeks ago, saying he couldn't wait to watch it with me.

"No, what?" he asked absently as he tossed his screwdriver into his tool bag.

I felt a ripple of disappointment. How could he *not* remember? It was one of the things we looked forward to most each year.

Last year for my birthday, Dad and I had flown down to Fort Myers to watch it in person. "The Sox have their spring training kick-off game tonight at JetBlue Park? Against the Minnesota Twins? I was going to turn it on downstairs."

"Oh, right." Dad wiped his forehead. "Look, *anjinho*, I know I promised to watch the game with you, but I need to finish this crib, *and* I promised Gail that I'd help Destry study for her Algebra 2 test tomorrow. Her grade's not great, and she's been struggling—"

"What about my grades?" Destry demanded, walking into the room. Her eyes glittered defensively.

I gave her my friendliest smile. "Dad was just telling me that you have an Algebra exam tomorrow. Maybe I can help you study. I'm taking Algebra 2 this year, too."

"Of course you are," Destry muttered. "Being the stellar student that you are and all." She did *not* mean it as a compliment.

Brush it off, I chanted, determined to prove to Dad that Destry and I were making headway with each other. I pushed on cheerfully, "We're probably on the same unit, and—"

"I don't need your help."

I flinched at her clipped, harsh tone, and my determination wavered. I replayed my offer in my head, wondering how I'd misstepped. Maybe she was insulted because I was a year behind her in school but was taking the same level for math. But I hadn't meant it to sound condescending. My face flushed. "Okay, no problem." My voice was small and tight. I walked toward the door. "I'm going downstairs. The game is about to start."

Dad gave me a sad, tired wave. "We'll catch the next game together. I promise."

I smiled and nodded, but my heart puddled miserably as I headed downstairs. For Dad's sake, I wanted to make peace with Destry. But brushing off her biting remarks was getting harder with each passing day, especially with Dad so preoccupied. Dad wanted me to make room for Destry and Gail in my life, but . . . what if he couldn't make room for me in his?

Chapter Five

"Romeo *hasn't* forgotten his Frog Princess. Not even close."

Those were the first words out of Kyan's mouth when I found him pacing in front of my locker on Monday morning. Viv was there, too, smiling and bouncing lightly on her tiptoes with excitement.

"What are you talking about?" I asked.

Viv held up a page from the *MinuteMan* and stabbed her finger into its center. My pulse jolted as I read the classified ad printed in big, bold caps:

PAUPER PAINTER SEEKS HIS MISSING PRINCESS
Looking for a Frog Princess, last sighted at Swoonful of

Sugar on Valentine's Day. Any information?

Stop by the *MinuteMan* pressroom ASAP!

I collapsed against my locker, trying to catch my breath. "Omigod." A smile swept across my face. "That means . . . he *has* been looking for me."

Viv squealed, gripping my hand and jumping up and down. "Isn't it just the most romantic thing you've ever seen?"

The thrill of it all made my head spin. "So . . . what should I do?"

"Well, you have your job interview at the *MinuteMan* during lunch period, right?" Kyan asked.

I nodded.

"So you go in for the interview, and while you're there, you tell them you're the Frog Princess."

"You find out Romeo's real name," Viv said, picking up where Kyan left off, "and you two are reunited." She snapped her fingers. "It's simple."

The paper shook in my hand as I reread the words in the ad. Questions filled my head. *What would I say when I told Romeo who I was? How would he react?* Excitement, and then dread, coursed through me.

I swallowed thickly. "What if he's disappointed when he finds out it's me? I mean, I was wearing a mask that night. What if he imagined I was drop-dead gorgeous? And then he sees me, and I'm . . ."

"Perfect," Viv said firmly. "Self-affirming statements are everything in modeling. You say it; you become it."

"*Plain* was more what I had in mind," I quipped with a nervous laugh.

"You're the same girl he hung out with on Valentine's Day," Kyan said. "Besides, if looks were all he cared about, would he have fallen for a mystery girl wearing a frog mask in the first place?"

"True enough." I laughed, but I still felt a quaking uncertainty. The first bell rang, and I quickly grabbed my books from my locker and waved good-bye to Kyan and Viv.

"See you in Biology," Kyan said as he headed down the hallway toward his Spanish class.

"Try not to obsess about it!" Viv called over her shoulder.

Yeah . . . right.

I spent the morning in a daze, vaguely nodding in my classes and pretending to take notes while every thought I had centered on my interview and the ad in my back pocket. Kyan elbowed me a dozen times during our Bio unit on photosynthesis, but then he gave up and let me go back to staring out the window at the frosty sky.

"Man, you're in bad shape," Kyan said as we left class. "You'd better go to the pressroom now."

I took a deep breath. "I don't know if I can do this."

"You better," Kyan said. "You and your Romeo are single-handedly keeping my faith in romance alive."

"But you said you and Viv are—"

"Never going to happen," Kyan said. "I remember what I said. But it's like believing in alien insects. It might be impossible, but I still don't want to hear they don't exist."

"Thanks a lot," I said drily. "Now I don't feel any pressure at all."

"Anytime." Kyan laughed. "Meet us at your locker after school?"

I nodded and headed nervously down the hall. When I walked into the pressroom, I smiled at the familiar storm of keyboards clicking manically to deadlines. Instantly, my pulse began hammering in time to their clatter. The surge of excitement I felt at the idea of working on a paper again was so intense, that I almost forgot the other reason I was here. Almost, but not quite.

I took a step farther into the room and a blonde girl with a no-nonsense look glanced up from her computer screen.

I gave her my winningest smile. "Hi, I'm Lise. I'm here for a job interview."

The girl rolled her eyes, then headed for the back of the room, giving me an abrupt, "Wait here."

"Okay," I said cheerily, unfazed by her don't-waste-my-time demeanor.

I watched as the girl tapped the shoulder of a boy bent over a lightboard. He was probably the editor-in-chief, checking photo proofs. I remembered doing that back at my old school.

"What?" the guy grumbled.

"You've got another victim," the girl quipped, jerking her head in my direction.

The boy shoved the photo loop across the lightboard, making the kids hovering around him start.

"They're no good," he said flatly. "Dump them and start over. You can do better."

The hover-kids exchanged disgruntled glances. "But the deadline—" one glasses-wearing girl started.

"Just . . . do it!"

The boy straightened and turned around, black curls framing his frowning face.

I gasped.

There were the angular features and those swoon-worthy green eyes. It was *him*! My Romeo.

My heart skittered as our eyes met. I lost my breath, hoping to see a flicker of recognition on his face. But there wasn't anything except the blank look of a stranger. Hopes . . . crash-landed.

He extended his hand, and heat zinged through my fingertips as they touched his. But he only gave me a firm, businesslike handshake.

"Hi. I'm Rajeev Batik, the editor-in-chief. You can call me Raj."

"Raj on a good day," snorted the blonde who'd first met me at the door. "Bossy McBoss-A-Lot on a bad."

Raj glared at her. "Chrissy, don't you have an Op-Ed to write?"

Chrissy walked away mumbling under her breath while Raj turned his focus back to me. "So, you're here about the reporting job?"

"Um, I . . . I . . ." *I'm your princess,* my heart screamed.

Raj blew out an exasperated breath. "Look, we're really busy here, and I've only got a few minutes."

I looked into his eyes, my head spinning with confusion and disappointment. I'd been daydreaming about this moment for so long, but now everything about it was wrong. Raj was brisk, unsmiling, and cold—not anything like the witty, sweet artist boy from Swoonful.

My mouth opened and closed like a suffocating fish's before it finally urped out, "Yes, I'm here for the job. I emailed my application last week. I've had a lot of experience with reporting."

Raj waved his hand impatiently. "Forget the application. That's school policy. What I'm interested in is your writing."

I nodded. "I sent in some samples—"

"Your writing *under pressure,*" he snapped, motioning for me to sit down at an empty computer station. "Lots of people can write well when they have time to prepare. But you won't have that luxury on deadline." He handed me some scribbled, cryptic notes, and a typed article titled, "Whitman Residents Debate Plan for Outlet Mall."

"This article was too awful to run," he said. "Rewrite it. You have twenty minutes."

I nodded. As I felt the weight of the paper against my palms, my bumbling nervousness vanished, replaced by an energizing swell of enthusiasm. My confusion over Raj changed into a fierce determination to prove to him how good I could be. Here was the sort of article I'd loved to write back in Boston—something with bite. I turned to the computer and started typing. My fingers flew, cozily at home on the keys as the cursor raced swiftly across the screen.

It seemed like only a minute later that Raj tapped my shoulder, saying, "Time's up."

I blinked, coming out of my writing daze to see my three-page masterpiece spitting out of the printer. Raj snapped it up before I had time to re-read the first sentence, and I held my breath as his eyes scanned the pages. Finally, he looked up, his expression stony.

"Clunky in spots, but not bad."

...ot believing my ears. "I barely had

"We'll give you a try," he said with resignation, as if he wished there were a better option available. "Articles are due every Monday morning by seven a.m. You're on the food beat."

"The food beat?" I was pretty sure steam was pouring out of my ears now. "But I used to be a features reporter. I was an editor-in-chief at my old school!"

Raj raised an eyebrow. "Not anymore. Take it or leave it."

He turned, already walking away, while my mouth hung open in shock. How could I have misread him so completely that night at Swoonful? I hadn't fallen for a kind, introspective artist. I'd fallen for a completely obnoxious jerk. Unless he had an evil twin or something, this made no sense.

I spun toward the door, ready to march out without ever seeing him again. But then I froze, remembering his disarming smile at Swoonful, how the green flecks in his eyes had danced in the candlelight. How his lips had been so close to mine.

A shivery thrill ran up my spine. What if that Raj was still in there? I straightened, lifting my head as I made my decision.

"I'll take the job," I said firmly.

Raj nodded. "Good. A new restaurant just opened up on Cobblestone Alley. It's called Thai Me to the Moon. Give it a try and write up a review. Due next Monday."

"There's one more thing," I blurted before he could turn away again. My heart drummed louder than a printing press. "It's about the ad for the missing princess."

Suddenly, his fierce demeanor cracked. "Do you know who she is?" he asked urgently, stepping closer. So . . . maybe he wasn't as tough as he seemed after all.

"I do." *It's me! It's me!* The truth was right there on the tip of my tongue, but I couldn't say it. Not yet. Not until I found out who the real Raj was. I thought quickly. "But the thing is she's . . . shy. If you give me your email address, I might be able to convince her to talk to you." A plan was beginning to form in my mind, a plan for how I might find out more about him without revealing who *I* was.

"Sure, sure." Raj hurriedly wrote down his email on a piece of paper and handed it to me. "But why doesn't she want to see me again?" He sighed in frustration, running his hand through his curly hair. "Can't you tell me anything else about her?"

"I can tell you one thing. She's looking forward to getting to know the real you." I smiled at his perplexed face before I turned to walk away.

Chapter Six

I finished my homework on the bus ride home, then inhaled my dinner so that I could have first dibs on the family computer to put my plan into action.

Please be online, I chanted in my head as I logged in using my brand-new email, FrogPrincess@webmail.com.

After filling Kyan and Viv in on what had happened with Raj, the three of us brainstormed, coming up with the idea of using my Frog Princess alias to talk to him. That way, I had time to solve the mystery of his Dr. Jekyll and Mr. Hyde routine without things getting too awkward. And, if the jerk side of him was permanent, I could end things without him ever knowing that the girl he'd just hired for the paper was also his missing princess.

I waited for my inbox to pop up, and when it did, my heart

jumped gleefully at the sight of the green "online" bubble next to RajBat@webmail.com. I held my breath and sent an invite for a live chat.

> **FrogPrincess:**
> Frog Princess seeking Pauper Painter. Are you there?

Within seconds, a reply came shooting back:

> **RajBat:**
> Hi! I can't believe it's you! I've been scouring the kingdom in search of you. After you left that night, I was worried I'd never find you again.

I smiled at the screen.

> **FrogPrincess:**
> Me too. If I'd known you worked on the school paper, you wouldn't have had to scour.

> **RajBat:**
> Sorry. I guess I forgot to mention it. It's not the best part of who I am.

> **FrogPrincess:**
> Yeah, I heard you were sort of . . . obnoxious today.

> **RajBat:**
> Obnoxious?!?

> **FrogPrincess:**
> Don't worry. I didn't believe it.

Nothing came back for a minute, and I started to worry that he'd left. But then:

RajBat:
I'm just trying to print the best paper possible. Your friend Lise needs to grow a thicker skin, or she won't be able to hack it.

I sat back in the chair, bristling. A thicker skin, huh? Well, we'd just see about that.

FrogPrincess:
Don't worry about her. She can take whatever you dish out. ☺
So . . . what are you up to? Painted any new masterpieces lately?

RajBat:
I wish. I haven't drawn anything new since Valentine's Day.

FrogPrincess:
Oh . . . lost your muse? ☺

RajBat:
Yes, I'm always inspired by frogs.

FrogPrincess:
As anyone would be. Ever wonder why Monet painted so many lily pads?

RajBat:
Quit making me laugh. I just dropped my charcoals all over my keyboard.

FrogPrincess:
Charcoals? I thought you hadn't drawn lately.

RajBat:
I was trying tonight. But it wasn't working.

FrogPrincess:
Maybe the problem is your subject. What were you trying to draw?

RajBat:
You.

My heart jolted, and I smiled at the screen.

FrogPrincess:
It's my webbed feet, right? They're tough to capture.

RajBat:
I want to draw the real you. But all I have to go on is the mask.

FrogPrincess:
Maybe it's better that way. Maybe I'm not what you hope I am under the mask.

RajBat:
I already know who's under there . . . the real you. But I'd like to see her too!

FrogPrincess:
You have seen her . . .

I typed the words, then deleted them before they got sent. I had to be careful not to give too much away.

I jumped as a hand tapped my arm, and I swiveled in my chair to see Destry peering over my shoulder.

"I have to get on there for a homework assignment," she said. Her eyes narrowed as she scanned the screen. "Who's RajBat?"

"Just a new friend from school," I said. "Can I have five more minutes?"

Destry crinkled her nose. The telltale sign of an oncoming temper tantrum. "I really need to . . . *now*. It's important."

"Fine," I mumbled, then typed a quick good-bye:

FrogPrincess:
Sorry, I have to go. Let's talk more later.

I hit SEND and was waiting for a response when Destry clicked the mouse, logging me out.

"Thank you," she sang happily, claiming the computer with a haughty smile. "I'll be done in ten."

Brush . . . it . . .off, I thought as I gritted my teeth.

And I did. For ten . . . twenty . . . thirty minutes, watching the time on the clock tick by as Destry giggled and blushed over whatever "homework" she was doing. Finally, an hour was up, and so was my patience. I walked over to the computer, and, as gently as I could, said, "Um, are you almost done?"

"Not quite," Destry said.

I peeked at the screen, and my frustration rapidly turned to fuming. "Hey!" I cried. "You've been on Twitter this whole time? You said you were doing homework!"

Destry shrugged. "Whatever." She locked eyes with me, as if daring me to say something else.

I glared at her. "You can't just monopolize the computer for socializing!" My voice was echoing through the family room now.

"Neither can you!" she said, her voice rising to match mine.

"Girls!" Gail came in from the kitchen, arching her back in a classic pregnancy waddle. She looked tired and uncomfortable, and I felt a momentary pang of guilt that she was being dragged into this. "What's the problem?"

"Lise was chatting with some guy, but I had homework to do." Destry molded her face into a practiced pout. "You always say schoolwork over social time, right, Mom?"

"That *is* the rule in this house, Lise," Gail said with a sigh.

"Sure!" I threw up my hands. "You expect *me* to follow it but not *her*!" I jabbed a finger toward Destry. "She was tweeting the entire time, but I get blamed while she gets away with everything! It's so unfair!"

"*Basta!* Enough!" Dad's voice was gruff. Still in his coat from work, he walked into the family room and slipped an arm protectively around Gail. "Lise. Destry. What's this all about?"

I started ranting the second Destry did, and our voices rose to an indecipherable yell. We were startled silent when Dad gave a deafening whistle, making a time-out signal with his hands.

"You know what?" He heaved a disgruntled breath. "It doesn't even matter what you were fighting about. It's obvious you two have gotten off on the wrong foot, and it's upsetting . . . for everyone." He gave Gail's belly a tender pat. "So. I'm giving you a job. You'll be painting the nursery. Together."

"But, Dad—" There was no way I was spending that much time with Destry. Nuh-uh.

Destry started to protest, too. "What? But I have ballet after school—"

Dad held up his hand. "You'll get started this weekend."

I swallowed down the rest of my arguments and nodded, willing to take the punishment if it meant erasing the disappointment I saw in Dad's face.

I hurried back to the computer, hoping to reconnect with Raj one more time before bed. He was offline, but my heart leapt when I saw an email from him:

To: FrogPrincess@webmail.com
From: RajBat@webmail.com
Hi again,
That's the second time you ran away without saying good-bye. Are you sure you're a Frog Princess and not Cinderella? (Just kidding.) But I am getting a little bit of a complex. (Not kidding.) How about

going ice skating with me? This Saturday at Revere
Pond at noon. Please say yes.

I couldn't stop the grin from spreading across my face. He was
asking me out! He wanted to see me again!

Blushing, I immediately typed a "See you there" reply, but the
second I hit SEND, my happiness screeched to a halt.

Wait a second. I'd just agreed to meet him in person! Or, er,
the princess had!

And Raj had already met me, Lise, at the pressroom that day,
and things hadn't gone so well between us.

How was I going to pull that off without revealing who I
was? Ugh.

How, how, how? I put my forehead in my hands to think.
Then I jumped up in a *eureka!* moment. I had the perfect answer.
I would be there on Saturday, and so would the princess. And I
knew exactly who she would be . . .

"*Me?*" Viv said, gawking at me from under her ludicrously
long lashes. "You want *me* to pretend to be *you*?"

"Not exactly. I'll be me. You be the Frog Princess." I smiled as she and Kyan shook their heads skeptically. We were eating lunch in the cafeteria while I shared last night's brainstorm with them. "We'll all go skating together. But *you're* going to pretend that you're the girl Raj met at Swoonful of Sugar. Just until I can get a legitimate read on him. You know, figure out who the real Raj is, and if I actually like him."

"But, Lise, we don't look anything alike," Viv said. "Don't you think he'll know right away that I'm not the girl he met that night?"

I shook my head. "It was dark in the patisserie, and I had on a mask. Besides, you and I both have brown eyes. And"—I shrugged—"you can tell him you were wearing a wig or something."

"He's not my type," Viv said.

"That's okay," I said. "You're supposed to find out if he's *mine*."

We giggled, but Kyan frowned. "I don't like it," he said. "You're messing with his heart *and* his head." It was the first contribution he'd made to the discussion. I got the distinct impression that he didn't like the notion of me involving Viv in this at all.

"It's only for a little while," I said. "If I decide that I like him, then we'll tell him the truth. If I don't like him, we'll end it with him."

"What about Holden?" Kyan asked Viv flatly. "Won't he be mad? I mean, you've been dating him practically a whole week now. For you, that's serious."

"Hey, that sounded kind of harsh," Viv said. She leaned her head against his shoulder playfully. "Why so grumpy today? Are you jealous?"

I knew Viv meant it as an innocent joke, since she was completely oblivious to Kyan's undying devotion to her. But I cringed, watching Kyan flounder in embarrassment. "No! Of course not! It's just . . . not really fair to him, right?"

Viv sighed. "I don't really care what Holden thinks. I'm so over him. He told me last night that I should lay off chocolate or I'd have to quit modeling. As if I don't hear that enough from my mom." She shrugged, then grinned slyly, opening her lunch satchel to reveal a mound of Hershey's Kisses. "Holden and Trent must have gotten their jerk diplomas together."

"Why do you go for guys like that?" I asked her.

"I don't know," Viv said, popping a chocolate into her mouth. "I guess because they keep asking me out, and they tell me I'm pretty. Every girl wants to get asked out and told she's pretty, right?"

"Yes," I acknowledged, "but if they turn out to be jerks, it's not worth it in the end. Which is why I need to find out more about Raj. So . . . will you do it?"

Viv smiled. "Sure. I guess it'll be fun."

But as Kyan and I said good-bye to Viv and headed for our lockers, Kyan kept his head down, frowning at the floor.

"Are you okay?" I asked. "'Cause you look miserable."

"I am," he said. He rubbed the top of his head so fiercely that I started to worry he might make a bald spot. "Like a cockroach sprayed with Raid."

"I . . . don't really get that," I said. "But it sounds bad."

He gaped at me. "It's horrible. All those bug nerves exploding in agony." My face must have been blank, because he gave up, sighing. "Never mind."

"Is this about Viv?" I asked as I grabbed my books from my locker.

"Of course it is!" he growled.

"I'm sorry. I should've checked with you to see if you'd mind before I asked for her help with Raj."

"No," Kyan said. "This isn't your fault. I'm the one who's been telling you all along that she can't ever be mine."

"That's true," I said. "The impossible alien insects thing, remember?"

"Well, of course I have to *say* that!" he cried. "It's how I protect myself. I mean, she sees every guy as potential dating material. But not me. Never me." He shook his head. "It's a hopeless case."

"No, it's not," I said. "You could tell her how you feel."

He rolled his eyes. "So she can do what? Laugh at me? No thanks. We're friends again for the first time since preschool. I can't ask for more."

"As long as you're okay with that," I said.

He nodded firmly. "I just forget every once in a while that I have to be."

I offered up an encouraging smile. "Hey, at least she's done with Holden. And you know nothing will ever happen between her and Raj. She said that already."

But Kyan still looked glum, and a worried crease appeared between his eyebrows. "Are you sure about this, Lise? What if your plan doesn't work the way you think it will?"

"Don't be such a doomsdayer," I said, slugging his arm as the bell rang. "What could possibly go wrong?"

· · ● ● ● · ●

"He's not coming," I said, double-checking my watch for the hundredth time as I wobbled unsteadily on my skates. I'd asked Kyan and Viv to meet me at Revere Rink a half an hour early, just to be on the safe side. I scanned the snow-covered park with its charming white gazebo and ice-tipped trees. A dozen skaters were already on the pond, their scarves whipping merrily behind them as they spun on the ice. New England charm wasn't something I saw much of back in Boston, although it was tough to enjoy it now with my nerves strung so tight.

"You said noon," Viv said distractedly, her head bent close to Kyan's over his smartphone screen. "Omigod, this YouTube video on termites is unbelievable. Do you know they eat through wood twice as fast if they're listening to Pink Floyd?"

Kyan beamed proudly. He lit up every time she showed an

interest in his world of bugs. And, surprising as it was, her interest seemed legit.

"No, I didn't," I said, trying not to get annoyed that neither one of them seemed worried that Raj was still nowhere to be seen. But after another five minutes of them tête-à-tête-ing over termites, I was officially annoyed. "Hey, guys!" I said. "A little moral support, here?"

Viv glanced up. "Okay, okay, sorry," she said, nudging Kyan to get him to pocket his phone. "We're a hundred percent here for you." She smiled encouragingly and bent to pull on her ice skates. "It's only twelve-oh-one, Lise. Trust me, he's not going to give up the chance to meet his soul mate."

"Yeah, which one of you is playing that part again?" Kyan mumbled sarcastically.

I was about to give him a scolding glance when I caught sight of Raj cresting the top of the hill. I grabbed Viv's arm. "He's here."

His curls were tumbling out from under his dark-green newsboy cap, and his untucked shirttails peeked out from under his corduroy barn jacket with a disheveled artistic charm. I smiled, my breath quickening, then immediately checked myself, remembering how he'd behaved in the pressroom.

Who will he be today? I wondered.

"He's *cute*, Lise," Viv whispered. "I never noticed before."

"Tell me about it," I said. Then, with a drumming heart, I waved to him. He stopped midstride as he recognized me, confusion passing over his features.

"Lise?" He walked closer. "Hi. Um, what are you doing here?"

My spirits sank. He didn't seem pleased to see me. Not even close. Was it because he thought *I* was the princess, and I wasn't anything like he'd hoped I would be? A quiver of pain shot through my chest, but I pushed it away with a smile.

"Hey," I said. "Viv asked me to come with her to meet you." I took a deep breath. "She's . . ."

"Your princess!" Viv said, giving a playful curtsy. "Surprise!"

Raj's expression morphed into a pleased perplexity. "Wow." He gave a nervous laugh. "Viv? I never guessed, I mean . . ." He smiled. "You're not who I expected."

"I hope that's a good thing." Viv smiled, putting a hand on her hip in a scolding, flirty gesture.

"No, I mean, yes," Raj stammered. "Yes, it's a good thing." He tilted his head quizzically. "Your hair looked so much darker that night at Swoonful."

"Of course." Viv's laugh was lilting and musical. "I forgot I was wearing a wig that night."

"Oh," Raj said haltingly. "And your voice . . ."

"She had a cough," I blurted, remembering my hoarse throat on Valentine's Day. "All better now!"

"Right." Raj fell into a stilted silence, glancing awkwardly at me and Kyan.

"I asked Lise and Kyan to come skating with us," Viv said smoothly, following his glance. "I was a little nervous about seeing you again."

"Really?" Raj said. "You don't seem nervous at all."

Truthfully, she didn't. She was exuding so much confidence that I could easily see where her modeling talent came from. She joked with him as he put on his skates, then slipped her arm smoothly through his to lead him onto the ice. She spun into the center of the rink, performing a flawless figure eight. Then she grabbed Raj's hand and swooped under it in a twirl that made him laugh and spin her faster.

"Come on, you two!" she called to Kyan and me as she and Raj breezed past. "While the pond's still frozen!"

Kyan gave me an uncertain glance, but I smiled to show him that I was fine with everything. Things were going exactly like I planned. Of course, that was until I slid onto the ice.

Or fell onto it, rather.

Ouch.

"Are you okay, Lise?" Kyan asked, skating up next to me. He looked sort of like a scrawny scarecrow balancing on stilts.

I planted my hands on the ice to hoist myself up to a standing position again. "I'm okay!" I said, embarrassed and praying that Raj hadn't seen. "Just a little rusty." I tried a simple glide and immediately landed on my backside.

Kyan helped me up. "Just how rusty are you?" he whispered.

I shrugged. "I haven't had much practice on skates. Like . . . no practice, actually."

"And I thought *I* looked ridiculous." He sighed, nodding his head toward Viv. "Just look at her. She would even be gorgeous picking her nose."

I wanted to argue with this declaration for the sake of cheering him up, but I glanced at her and knew he was right. Half the people on the pond had moved to the outskirts, admiring Viv's graceful movements on the ice. She was laughing and talking with Raj while he skated beside her. He still looked slightly surprised, as if he couldn't quite believe that she was actually the princess. But he was behaving like the perfect gentleman, holding her hands as they skated together, smiling as she playfully skated backward on the ice. And Viv was doing a fantastic job playing the role of princess. In fact, I couldn't have done it better myself.

A smidge of uncertainty nagged at my mind, but I pushed it away and shoved off across the ice. "Let's catch up with them," I called over my shoulder to Kyan, gaining confidence as my skates found a tentative rhythm. I gained speed as Raj and Viv grew larger in my sights. Maybe I could do this.

I . . . I couldn't stop!

"Look out!" I screeched a second before I slammed into Raj.

"Whoa there," he said, catching me around the waist as my feet flew out from under me. I opened my eyes to see his smiling face, inches from mine. There was absolutely nothing jerky about his face right now. Nothing but . . . *sigh* . . . total dreaminess. "Are you all right?"

"Um, yeah," I said when I found my breath, straightening with a nervous laugh. "Sorry. I think my skates are broken."

"Yup, that *must* be the reason," he said jokingly. "Here." He held out his hand. "Follow me. You *and* your two left feet."

We slid a few feet from Kyan and Viv, my hand tingling as he eased me across the ice. "See?" he said. "You don't need to try so hard."

"I'll fall," I said as he sped up a little.

He grinned. "Then I'll catch you." He glanced down at my feet. "Smooth out your gliding, so it's not so—"

"*Clunky?*" I quipped, raising an eyebrow. "Like my writing?"

A cloud of embarrassment passed over his face. "That may have been a little harsh," he admitted quietly. "But I expect my writers to do their best work."

"You must have pretty high standards," I said.

"I do," he said. "But I'm guessing you do, too." He studied my face. "I read your other writing samples after your interview. There wasn't a single typo in any of them. Maybe you're a little bit of a perfectionist?"

"Maybe," I said grudgingly.

"Then we'll make a good team," Raj said. "As long as you can handle my constructive criticism."

"I can," I said staunchly, then added, "As long as there's a valid reason for it."

"If it makes you feel any better, I'm my own worst critic. I've tossed tons of my own work before."

"Your articles?" I asked.

"No. My artwork."

"Oh, yeah," I said. "Viv told me how much you love art. So . . . why would you throw your work away?"

He shook his head. "Sometimes I worry I'm not good enough to be able to really do something with it."

I gaped at him. "That's ridiculous!" I cried. "Your art's incredible!"

He looked puzzled. "You've never seen it."

Oops. "No," I said cautiously, hating that I had to lie. "But . . . from what Viv told me, I'm sure it is."

"Some people I know think it's a waste."

"Really?" I said. "Who?"

His brow furrowed, and he opened his mouth to say something else, but then Viv swooped in between us, laughing, with Kyan at her side.

"Hey, guys, we've been out here forever," she said. "How about we break for hot chocolate? My fingers are going numb."

"Here." Raj took her hands, cupping them in his own, then gently blew on them. "Better?"

My stomach dropped.

"Yeah," she said quietly, her voice lifting in surprise at the gesture. "Thanks." She looked at him with a sudden shyness I'd never seen in her before, her cheeks blossoming into a blush. I felt a pang of jealousy, but just then my cell phone rang. When I saw Destry's name on the caller ID, the jealousy was replaced by panic. I didn't even need to pick up the phone to know why she was calling.

"Oh, no!" I said, checking the time. "I forgot I'm supposed to help Destry paint the nursery. I'm an hour late!" I clumsily lurched off the rink with everyone following. "We'll have to save the hot chocolate for another day."

Viv hesitated. "Or . . . the rest of us could stay," she suggested, glancing at Raj, who was nodding enthusiastically.

"I'm up for more skating," he said, a little too quickly.

"I'm out," Kyan said, his face pinching. "I think the skates gave me blisters."

Raj looked at Viv, smiling bashfully. "It's the two of us then."

The two of them. My heart gave a confused lurch as I watched them smiling at each other. It was tough to tell if Viv's smile was part of the show she was putting on, or if she was genuinely happy. Suddenly, the last thing in the world I wanted was to leave the two of them alone together. But then Viv gave me a subtle nod and wink, as if she were saying, *Go on. I've got everything under control.*

"Okay," I said, reluctantly slipping into my boots and turning to Viv. "Call me later?"

"Sure," Viv said, but she and Raj were already waving as they headed for the snack shack at the edge of the pond.

Kyan and I started for home together, but he couldn't walk as fast as I needed to because of his blisters, so I finally said good-bye and took off at a jog, hoping to get home before Destry completely freaked. I didn't think the odds were in my favor.

My chest ached as the frigid air blew in and out of my lungs, but I wasn't sure it was from the cold. Every time I thought about Viv alone with Raj in full flirt mode, the ache got stronger. I'd been so sure nothing could go wrong, and on the surface, nothing had. Viv and Raj had gotten along great. No, *perfectly*. And that, I thought with a sigh, could be a perfectly awkward problem.

Chapter Seven

"You're late!" Destry snapped when I walked into the nursery, out of breath and stripping off my coat and hat.

"I lost track of time," I said, picking up a paint roller.

"Yeah, well, we'd better be finished by five." She handed me a tray of paint. "I'm supposed to go bowling tonight with Jake, but your dad says I can't until we're done with this stupid project."

I nodded in agreement. The less time I had to spend in a confined space with Destry, the better. I headed for the corner of the room farthest from where she was working and began rolling the paint onto the wall. It fanned out in a pretty pale teal, and I smiled to myself. Gail had gone with my color suggestion after all. No wonder Destry was so grumpy.

"Not like *that*," she said, shaking her head at my work. "You're using too much paint. See? It's dripping down the wall."

I stepped back, my temper flaring. "I don't see any drips." I so did *not* need a lesson in room painting from her right now.

She gave a disgruntled sigh. "Let me show you. Give me the roller." She reached for it, but I instantly jerked back, and a thin stream of paint dribbled off the roller and onto Destry's jeans.

"Omigod!" she shrieked. "Look what you did! These are my favorite pair of jeans!"

I stared at her, seeing red. Forget brushing it off. It was time to let her have it.

"So what?" I said. "Your wardrobe could use a little downsizing anyway." I flicked my wrist, and a spray of paint flew off my roller and splattered across the front of her shirt. "Oops."

Her mouth dropped open as fury purpled her face. "You," she seethed, dipping a paintbrush in her bucket, "did that on purpose." She flicked a fountain of paint from her brush, hitting me squarely in the face.

I felt a moment of shock before I acted again.

"And I enjoyed it!" I cried, grabbing my own brush and boldly slathering paint across her cheek. "I'm so sick of the way you treat me!" I added as she slapped her paintbrush down my arm.

She screeched as I tossed the paint from my tray in a wave over her hair. Now we were both flinging paint blindly, splattering it across each other as fast as we could.

"I never asked you to move in," she cried, wiping paint from her eyes. "I never asked you to share my room. I never had a say in any of it! I hate it! I hate—"

You. That was the word teetering on her lips, I was sure. But she never got to say it, because Dad walked in.

There was a clatter as Destry's paintbrush dropped from her hand. Or, maybe the clatter was Dad's jaw hitting the floor. I couldn't be sure, but my bet was on Dad.

"*Ay meu Deus!* What are you doing?" It wasn't a question so much as a roar.

The room looked like a paintball war zone.

"It's her fault!" Destry sputtered, turning on an impressive display of waterworks. "I was painting by myself because *she* was out with her friends. She forgot all about it, and then she finally shows up and dumps paint all over me!"

"That is a lie!" I cried.

"Stop!" Dad held up a hand, glaring at us. "I don't care who did what. Both of you need to start thinking less about yourselves and more about your family."

"This ... is not *my* family!" I cried, hurling my roller onto the floor as all the built-up frustrations of the last few weeks erupted. "It's yours! And ... and I don't belong here! I never will!"

A stricken look hit Dad's face. Destry stared from me to him, the fury on her face deflating in awkward silence. I felt tears welling up in my eyes. I hadn't meant to hurt Dad.

"You're both grounded until you fix this," Dad finally mumbled wearily. "This nursery is going to look beautiful, and you don't leave this house again until it does."

Dad left the room without another word, and before I gave Destry the satisfaction of seeing a single tear fall, I ran out, too.

That night, I punched my pillow and flipped over, trying to get comfortable. The sad fact was that some couches were made for sleeping, and Dad's and Gail's *wasn't* one of them. I sighed and burrowed deeper into the blankets, my stomach twisting as I replayed my fight with Dad in my head . . . again.

After sitting through an abysmal dinner in which the only sounds were of silverware scraping plates and food being swallowed, Dad and Gail had left to go to a birthing class at the hospital. Then Destry and I had retreated to separate corners of the house.

I'd set up camp on the couch in the den, because there was no way I was sleeping in the same room as Destry after everything that had happened. There was only one thing keeping me from calling Mom to beg for a ticket on the next plane to Switzerland: Raj. Every time I thought about his hands on my waist, catching me before I fell, a thrill went through me. I'd caught a glimpse of the same sweetness in him I'd seen that night at Swoonful. But he'd slipped into his know-it-all routine a few times, too. Even after skating, I was no closer to figuring him out than I had been before.

It didn't help that I hadn't heard a peep from Viv since we'd said good-bye at the rink. I'd texted and called her to find out what had happened after I left, but she hadn't answered. I didn't know why I was worried. I mean, she'd done exactly what I'd asked her to do! And I was grateful. Wasn't I? Only, if I was grateful, then why did my stomach twist each time I thought of Raj smiling at her as they skated, arm in arm?

Giving up on sleep, I got off the couch and sat down at the computer, logging on. I smiled when I saw Raj online, too. Within seconds, I got an invite from him for a live chat.

RajBat:
There you are. I was hoping you'd feel like talking.

FrogPrincess:
I'm here. Can't sleep. Family drama.

RajBat:
Uh-oh. What happened?

Frog Princess:
The usual. Do you ever feel like no one in your family really gets you?

RajBat:
Only every day. My family thinks I'm this person they can make into whoever they want. But I only feel like myself when I'm doing my art. And I never let them see that side of me.

FrogPrincess:
Why not?

RajBat:
My dad. He thinks art is a colossal waste of time. He's a county judge, and he's friends with Principal Hinkle. He helped get me the job as the newspaper's editor-in-chief so that I could strengthen my writing skills. He's hoping I'll go to law school someday. You know, follow in his footsteps or something.

FrogPrincess:
But . . . wouldn't you be happier doing what you loved?

RajBat:
It's not my choice to make.

FrogPrincess:
It stinks getting stuck with parental choices.

RajBat:
But hey, at least we got to go skating today, before all your drama. Right?

FrogPrincess:
It was the best part of my day.

RajBat:
For me, too. But I got frostbite on the way home.

FrogPrincess:
From what?

RajBat:
You forgot my great act of chivalry already? Yeesh. See if I loan you my jacket again the next time you spill hot chocolate all over yours.

I bit my lip. Viv had worn Raj's jacket home? That was . . . unexpected. But if she'd spilled hot chocolate, she would've had to. It made perfect sense. Of course it did.

FrogPrincess:
Thanx for the jacket, valiant Sir Raj. I hope the frostbite isn't serious. Don't want it messing with your painting hands.

RajBat:
Frozen fingers give me a very Picassoesque style. I'm going with it.

I heard the front door open and the sound of Dad's and Gail's voices in the hall.

FrogPrincess:
Uh-oh. Parental alert. Have to go.

RajBat:
Already? See u Monday. Goodnite.

I signed off and leapt for the couch, managing to get under the covers just as Dad and Gail tiptoed into the kitchen. I held my breath, wondering if they'd buy my fake sleep act. I heard Gail whisper that she was going upstairs, and an eternity seemed to pass in silence. Then, there were nearing footsteps, and I cringed, expecting another lecture. But there was only the soft touch of Dad planting a quick kiss on the top of my head.

I sagged into the couch as soon as he left, guilt washing over me. Except for my chat with Raj, I'd spent all night wishing that I could be back in Boston, in my own bedroom, in my own home, living my real life again. But then, Dad's love for me was as real as everything else in my life. I just didn't know if it was enough for me to stay.

I ran the paint roller over the wall, covering the last stark patch of white, then took a step back to admire my work. Not bad.

The walls were now covered with a smooth coat of teal, and I'd touched up the ceiling with white paint to cover up the last remnants of yesterday's war. I was taking the tarps off the crib and rocking chair when Destry walked in, still in her pajamas and yawning.

She stared at the room, blinking in surprise. "You . . . finished?"

I nodded. "It's almost noon, and I woke up early anyway."

More like, I never went to sleep. I'd spent most of the night tossing restlessly on the couch, thinking about Dad and Gail, and Mom, and Destry, and Raj and Viv. When Dad and Gail tiptoed past me early in the morning on their way out to run errands, I'd finally given up on sleep. I'd gone upstairs to work on the nursery, just to distract myself. At least the room was painted now, and I'd saved myself the awkwardness of having to work with Destry.

"It looks good," Destry said. "Um . . . thanks." She sounded surprisingly sincere, even if the words came out reluctantly.

I shrugged. "I didn't want to spend all day grounded. I figured you didn't, either."

Destry snorted. "That's for sure." She tilted her head, studying my face. "Hey, were you crying in the bathroom yesterday? I thought I heard you in there, and your eyes are totally red."

"No," I said quickly, ducking my head, knowing full well that my tear-sapped eyes were super puffy. "I think it's just . . . paint fumes."

"Whatever you say," she said doubtfully, turning toward the door. "You don't have to tell me."

I stared at her. Was I imagining it, or had there been the tiniest bit of hurt in her voice? Did that mean she *wanted* me to tell her?

I opened my mouth. "I—"

"Your dad and my mom are back. Mom was craving chocolate chip pancakes, so she made some for brunch." Destry was already moving down the hallway when she added, "Better come while they're still hot."

"'Kay," I mumbled. One thing about Destry's windows of opportunity: If they existed at all, which I still doubted, they didn't stay open for long.

As the mouthwatering smell of fresh-cooked pancakes wafted

up the stairs, I hurried to close the lids on the paint cans. Then my cell rang. My heart leapt. It was Viv! Finally!

"Hey!" I answered. "I tried calling you tons of times."

"I know," she said. "I'm so sorry. When I got home from the rink, my mom lit into me about letting my cheeks get chapped. She made me wear this avocado moisturizing mask for hours. Every time I tried to talk, I got the mask in my mouth. It was disgusting." I laughed, but she sighed. "I'm so sick of her rants about skin care. I swear, she'd keep me in a big plastic bubble if she could."

I felt bad for Viv, but wanted to hear the details on Raj. "So . . . how was the rest of skating? Fun?"

"Yeah, it actually was." She sounded surprised. "I mean, Raj is sort of . . . intense. And when he started talking about some art thing called Cubism, I thought he meant art *from* Cuba. So he lost me a little there. But he's the nicest guy, Lise. I don't know where you're getting this jerk stuff from. Raj is . . . sweet and smart and polite." She cleared her throat. "He even loaned me his jacket when I spilled cocoa on mine!"

"Yeah, he mentioned that," I said, feeling the same unease I'd felt at the rink. "We IM'ed last night."

"You did? That's great! Did he . . . did he say he had a good time?"

"It seemed like he did," I said.

"Well, that's a relief! We're so different. I can totally see how you hit it off with him, but I wasn't sure how we'd get along. Guys can be so . . . disappointing, you know? But he never acted bored when I talked, like Trent used to. And he's not a chronic burper like Holden. So those are pluses, right?"

"Definitely." I laughed. "I'd never go for a burper."

"There you go," she said. "That's *my* problem. I can never tell a bad boy from a good. Well, except for yesterday . . ." Her voice faded, and I sensed a strange moment of discomfort between us. But a second later she blurted out, "Guess what? He talked about you, after you left."

My pulse quickened. "He did?"

"Yeah. He said you seemed really smart, and you were probably the right choice for the reporting job."

A frown pulled at the corners of my mouth. *Probably* the right choice? That wasn't exactly a glowing compliment.

"He said one more thing, too, but . . ." Viv hesitated. "I'm not sure you're going to like it."

My grip tightened on the phone as my heart fluttered nervously. "What?"

"He said . . . that you liked to argue, and he wasn't sure you could be a team player at the paper." She blew out a breath.

"What is he talking about? *He's* the only person I argue with," I cried, strangling the phone. "And I'm a *great* team player!"

"Please don't be mad at me," Viv implored. "I promised I'd tell you everything, so I did."

"I'm not mad at you," I said. "I just can't believe he said that! I had this awesome chat with him last night, but now you tell me this!" I gave a frustrated *harrumph* into the phone. "Wait until he sees my first review. I'm going to knock his stuck-up socks off . . ." I gasped in panic, slapping a hand to my forehead. "Oh . . . no. I forgot."

"What?" Viv asked.

"My review of Thai Me to the Moon," I said weakly. "It's due tomorrow."

"Don't panic. It's only noon."

"I have to go," I said. "I haven't even been to the restaurant yet! I need to get over there right now."

"Wait a sec." Viv's words rushed out. "So . . . are you going to tell him the truth? You know, about who you are?"

"Not yet," I said. "I want to turn in my review first. I have to prove him wrong. I mean, he's passing these judgments about me, and he hasn't even given me a chance at the paper! I'm starting to think I don't get him at all."

"I don't know, Lise." Viv sounded doubtful. "He's got strong opinions, but . . . so do you. He seems pretty perfect. For you, I mean."

"We'll see." I said good-bye to Viv and hurried downstairs to grab my coat and ask Dad if I could take a rain check on pancakes. For a minute he looked as though he was going to argue, but then his face pinched, probably from a flashback of last night's fight, and he let me go.

I hurried outside, wrapping my scarf tighter around my neck as a crisp wind whipped through the streets. With my ThinkPad tucked safely into my tote, I scurried through the Sunday-sleepy neighborhood and, after just a few minutes, arrived in Whitman's small downtown.

Main Street was surprisingly quiet, with only a handful of

people window-shopping, cups of coffee in their gloved hands. Within seconds, I realized why. Almost all of the shops were closed. I felt a pang as I passed Swoonful of Sugar, which wouldn't open for a couple more weeks, I knew. The shop next door, a bookstore, was shuttered, too. I swallowed thickly, picking up the pace as a worrying thought crossed my mind. Worry swiftly became panic when I turned the corner onto Cobblestone Alley. The sign on the front window of Thai Me to the Moon spelled out my doom: CLOSED.

Oh . . . crud! I put my face to the window, peering inside at the funky, East-meets-West décor—the vibrant crimson lanterns, the gold-winged griffin-like creature painted on the wall. I imagined the humiliation I'd feel confessing what had happened to Raj. He'd gloat, for sure, and then fire me before I even wrote a single word. Not a chance I was going to let that happen. I'd just have to improvise, that's all.

I pulled up the restaurant's website on my cell, hoping they'd have a menu posted, but the menu page was under construction. Another strikeout. *Never mind*, I told myself firmly. *You can do this.*

I headed for home with growing confidence. I'd probably eaten at a dozen Thai restaurants in Boston. I knew the most popular dishes. I'd name-drop a few of them in my review, and no one would ever know. Especially Raj. When tomorrow morning rolled around, I'd hand in a terrific piece. I'd prove to him that I wasn't *probably* the right choice for the job. I was the perfect one.

Chapter Eight

I stood outside the pressroom, rereading the opening of my review one more time:

Stuck in the winter doldrums? Tired of your mom's crockpot stews? Wake up those hibernating taste buds with a journey through the exotic dishes at Thai Me to the Moon. You don't need your passport to experience the delicious, foreign flavors of Whitman's newest restaurant. The tom yum goong, hot and sour soup with shrimp and lemongrass, zings over your tongue like a sunshiny spring day. And the royal Massaman curry, with its sweet coconut tamarind sauce, savory potatoes, and roasted peanuts, is the perfect comfort food to shake off those wintry chills . . .

I smiled as I read to the end of the review. Sure, it wasn't the sort of provocative piece I loved to write, but still, it wasn't too shabby. It was clean, typo-free, and I'd even thrown in a few funny food puns for good measure. Most important, I'd made sure there wasn't a chance Raj would find anything wrong with it.

I walked into the pressroom with my head held high. Then I stopped short at the sight of Viv laughing and chatting with Raj, their heads bent together over a photo Viv was holding.

"Hey," I said hesitantly.

Viv's head snapped up in surprise, and the faintest blush spread over her cheeks. "Oh . . . hey!" she said cheerfully. "What are you doing here?"

I smiled, deciding to play it off lightly. "I work here, remember?" I said teasingly. "What about you?" I asked, trying to sound as casual as I could.

"Oh, I stopped by to give Raj his jacket back," she said breezily.

"Thankfully *before* I froze," Raj said, smiling at her as if they were sharing some hilarious secret.

"Okay . . . well . . . This is the Thai Me to the Moon piece," I blurted, handing the pages to Raj.

Raj nodded. "Thanks. If it's adequate, it'll run in the paper tomorrow."

Adequate? Seriously? "Well, I've got to head to English," I said, trying to keep the frustration out of my voice. "We have that test today on the Transcendentalists."

Viv groaned. "Don't remind me. All those essays on nature . . . I'm dying of boredom."

"Really?" Raj looked slightly disappointed. "I love Thoreau."

"Me too," I said. "And I guess we're going to see his grave when we visit Louisa May Alcott's house in Concord next week."

"Ick," Viv said. "Why does hanging out in a graveyard constitute a field trip? It gives me the creeps."

"I think it'll be awesome," Raj said with a hint of defensiveness. "Graveyards can be beautiful. You'll see." His face brightened. "Hey! We should sit together on the bus ride. I'll bring my favorite book of Transcendentalist poetry. Maybe I can change your mind."

"I doubt it. I'm not a literature sort of girl. That's Lise's specialty. You should talk to her about it sometime."

"Oh." Raj's voice dropped as he looked at me. "Right."

Viv glanced at me hesitantly, then said, "But, um, sure . . . all of us can sit together. You, Lise, me, and Kyan. It'll be fun!"

The bell rang, and I shouldered my book bag. "We've gotta go," I said to Viv, but she didn't move from Raj's side until I added, "Viv . . . are you coming?"

"Oh, yup!" she said, giving Raj a wave and a smile. "See you later!"

I turned sharply toward the door, feeling a sudden irritation. "We're going to be late to class," I said to Viv, "and I have my test."

She raised her eyebrows. "Sorry," she said. "You could've gone ahead without me."

"That's okay," I mumbled as we hurried through the halls toward my English class. "I wanted to walk with you," I added more kindly, feeling a stab of guilt at snapping at her. What was my problem? Why was I so annoyed with Viv, when she hadn't done anything?

When we reached my class, Viv gave me an encouraging

smile. "I'd wish you luck, but you don't need it. You'll ace the test." She started to turn away, then hesitated. "Lise?" She looked at me in a bashful way that was completely unlike her usual graceful poise and confidence. "You know that Raj and I are just friends, right? And I'm only trying to help you . . ."

"You *are* helping," I said, feeling my cheeks heating up. "Everything's fine."

She smiled in relief as she walked away. But as I sat down at my desk, I felt my insides squirming restlessly. It was the feeling you get when something's not right, but you can't quite put your finger on what it is.

Even after I'd finished my English test, pretty sure that I'd done well, the feeling stayed with me. I couldn't seem to shake it.

It followed me through the rest of the day, and by the time I'd finished a dinner of stilted silence with Dad, Gail, and Destry, my thoughts were a tangled knot of threads. My fight with Dad was one knot, my confusion about Raj another. In the middle of it all was a snapshot of Viv and Raj, bent over that photo in the pressroom, smiling at each other.

After I finished my homework, I logged on to the family computer. Part of me hoped Raj would be online, waiting, while another part hoped he wouldn't be, so my heart would be spared more confusion. My heart, as it happened, was out of luck.

> **RajBat:**
> Hey you. I found the perfect Transcendental quote for you. Ready?

> **FrogPrincess:**
> I'm on the edge of my seat.

> **RajBat:**
> "Beware of all enterprises that require new clothes."

I laughed out loud as I read, then quickly typed a response.

> **FrogPrincess:**
> Hey, was that a jab at modeling?

> **RajBat:**
> Who me? Never! Blame it on Thoreau. I think you've got great clothes, even if they are uber new.

> **FrogPrincess:**
> Yeah, well, I've got one for you. "To be yourself in a world that is constantly trying to make you something else is the greatest accomplishment." Ralph Waldo Emerson.

> **RajBat:**
> You're not very subtle, are you?

> **FrogPrincess:**
> I'm better at straight talk.

> **RajBat:**
> I thought you hated Transcendentalism, and now you're giving advice with it?

Yikes, I thought. I guess I messed that one up. I wasn't that convincing spouting Emerson as Viv.

FrogPrincess:
Well, I guess that quote stuck with me because it made me think of you.

RajBat:
So you're admitting it. You . . . think about me?

FrogPrincess:
Hmmm . . . maybe a little.

RajBat:
Ouch. What would it take to get to a lot?

FrogPrincess:
Just . . . be yourself, and you'll get there. ☺

RajBat:
Hmmm, I may not like Emerson that much anymore.

FrogPrincess:
LOL. Hey, I can't sleep (again). Got any music recommendations for transcending?

RajBat:
Try Chopin or Debussy. My painting music.

I logged in to my iTunes account, smiling at Raj's recommendations.

FrogPrincess:
Okay. Uploading playlists now. Will you listen with me?

RajBat:
I'd love to. Give me five minutes to get to my room.

FrogPrincess:
Me too . . . Good night.

RajBat:
Sweet dreams, Princess.

I logged off and hurried upstairs, then crawled into bed and slipped my earbuds in. Exactly five minutes after I'd said good night to Raj, I hit PLAY. Soft, sweet music filled my ears. I smiled, picturing Raj somewhere out there in the darkness, listening, too. As I drifted off, I was finally able to hit the *off* switch on my tangled-up brain. I listened to Raj's painting music, letting it lull me to sleep and stream through my dreams.

● ● ● ● ●

If Tuesday morning had a headline, it would read: LISE SANTOS IGNORES WARNING SIGNS; DISASTER STRIKES.

By disaster, I mean the never-want-to-show-your-face-at-school-again kind.

I saw Raj come barging out of the school's main office, a pile of *MinuteMan* issues under his arm, every muscle in his face and neck taut with anger.

"Hi—" I started, but didn't get any further than that. His eyes honed in on mine, darkening, and he swiftly took my arm, steering me down the hall.

"Pressroom," he muttered. "*Now*."

"What's the matter?" I sputtered, disoriented by his bizarre behavior. When his only answer was a disgusted shake of his head, my temper flared. He wasn't even telling me what the problem was! I pulled my arm from his grip. "I can walk by myself," I said, just as we reached the pressroom.

"Really?" he said, slapping one of the issues down on my desk. "Because you seem to have trouble writing unsupervised, so I wasn't sure about walking."

"What are you talking about?" I demanded, fighting to keep my focus on him without letting his cuteness distract me.

"Page five," he snapped. "Your review of Thai Me to the Moon?" He flipped through the issue, then stabbed a finger at the middle of a page. "It's great. Fantastic. Especially the part where you talk about the royal Massaman curry." He leaned closer, the green in his eyes sparking like jade flames. "That's not even on the restaurant's menu!"

Clammy dread slinked up my spine. Oh, this was bad. Very, very bad. "I—I—" My face was a furnace of embarrassment as I struggled to speak. I stared at the floor. "The thing is," I finally eked out, "when I went to the restaurant on Sunday, it was closed. I . . . I didn't . . . actually have a chance to try the food yet."

Raj threw the paper back on the desk. "That's obvious. And I suppose you didn't know that the restaurant was owned by Principal Hinkle's wife?"

"What?" I said weakly, barely able to speak over the roaring sound of my academic career getting flushed down the toilet.

"That's right." Raj scowled. "Mrs. Hinkle was born in Thailand. She's wanted to open a restaurant here for years."

Omigod. Of all the assignments to blow off, I'd chosen *this* one? What was wrong with me? "I didn't know . . ."

"*She* was one of the first people to read the issue this morning." Raj sighed, running a hand through his hair. "And *I* just spent the last twenty minutes in Principal Hinkle's office trying to apologize for your laziness."

"I'm *not* lazy!" I blurted. "How was I supposed to know that Whitman turns into a ghost town on Sundays? In Boston, restaurants are open every day!"

"That's no excuse," Raj said, shaking his head. "As a reporter, you're supposed to do your research, use time management. You had a week to eat there, and you waited until the last minute! You were at the rink with us on Saturday when you should've been working on the story!"

I glowered at him. He'd made it sound like going ice skating was a crime! "Well . . . I'm entitled to a social life, you know. And a restaurant review is *not* a story," I said emphatically. "I told you from the beginning that food isn't what I want to write about." I sighed. "I want to report on current events, student government—"

Raj scoffed. "After what you did? What makes you so sure that you're even a reporter on this paper?"

My heart slammed against my ribcage. Was he actually going to fire me? "I—I—"

"You think you're above writing about food," he said, turning away. "You're never going to get assigned a different beat if you keep up the attitude."

Relief poured over me, and I took my first breath in the last few minutes. "So . . . that means . . . I'm still on staff?"

"For now," he said grudgingly. "But you have to write an apology to Thai Me to the Moon. Today. We'll print it in the next issue and hope that Principal Hinkle and his wife forget about this."

"Fine," I said flatly, as the first bell rang. I wanted to rail at him, to tell him how unfair he was being. But one of the cardinal rules of reporting was "Seek truth and report it." I'd broken it, and now I had to follow journalism's hardest rule. I had to "Be accountable." It wouldn't be pretty, but every journalist has to eat some crow sooner or later. "I'll have it for you by the end of the day."

I turned toward the door just as Raj's cell rang. His hello when he answered was contracted and resigned. I chanced a look back at him and was surprised to see every ounce of confidence erased from his face.

"I know, Dad," he was saying as he rubbed his forehead, frowning. "I should've caught it before it went to press. It was a mistake. But I already talked to Principal Hinkle about it, and I'm going to fix it."

I paused, trying to figure out his end of the conversation. Was he talking about my review? If he was, then I guessed that Principal Hinkle must've called Raj's dad to tell him. So I'd managed to get Raj in trouble with his dad, too. Great. Guilt stabbed me as I watched him. I'd never seen him look so off-balance before, his usual self-assuredness replaced with worry.

When he hung up a second later, his face was miserable. He caught my eye, and I waited, holding my breath, wanting him to say something that would turn him back into that sweeter, softer Raj of macarons and moonlight.

"You're lucky you're friends with Viv," he snapped. "Otherwise, you wouldn't be getting a second chance."

The words stung. Maybe I was wrong to cling to the hope of a different Raj. Maybe the sweeter, softer guy I'd known that Valentine's night didn't really exist at all.

● ● ● ● ●

Kyan and Viv were in the middle of a heated debate over the killer instincts of female praying mantises when I found them in the cafeteria at lunchtime.

"I will never understand why a female mantis has to eat her mates alive," Kyan was saying. "She uses them, then kills them. It's cruel."

"I don't know," Viv was arguing. "If she has boyfriends like the ones I've had, they probably deserved it."

"You say that, but as we speak you're scouring the school for a date to Winter Formal. Meanwhile, Raj is thinking *you* like *him*. Isn't that cruel, too?"

"No," Viv said simply. "I can't go to the dance alone." She said *alone* like it was a repulsive disease of some kind. "Besides, Raj will end up going with Lise, once she tells him who she is." Her face clouded for the briefest second, then brightened with a photo-ready smile. "See? It'll all work out."

"No, it won't. I'll never go to the dance with Raj." I plunked down my lunch bag and announced decisively, "It's over."

"Wait . . . did it ever actually start?" Kyan said jokingly, but when he saw I couldn't even crack a smile, he grew solemn. "Sorry. What happened?"

"What didn't," I said glumly. Kyan and I had had a lab test in Bio earlier, so I hadn't had a chance to fill him in on the disaster with Raj. As I spilled the whole story, Kyan nodded sympathetically, adding in a few "unbelievables" for good measure. Viv, though, stared at her food, staying uncharacteristically silent. I finished with a sigh. "I'm done with this whole Frog Princess thing. He's not the person I thought he was. And thank goodness he'll never know who I really was."

"But still . . . that stinks," Kyan agreed. "I mean, what happened between you guys on Valentine's Day seemed like the real deal."

"I thought so, too," I said regretfully as I took a bite of my sandwich. "Sometimes when we chat online, it's like we're back at Swoonful all over again. But in the pressroom, he's a complete jerk. I can't stand him like that."

"But . . . you don't really think he's a jerk," Viv said softly. "I mean, he *was* right. You shouldn't have fudged your review."

Kyan and I both stared at her. "You're kidding." I gave a short, uncomfortable laugh. "I shouldn't have fudged it, but *come on*. He didn't have to get on such a high horse. He could've handled the whole thing differently."

Viv nodded. "Maybe, but . . . it wasn't his fault. You could've said you were sorry."

"To *him*?!?" I rolled my eyes. "No way."

She squirmed in her seat. "Hey, I don't get why he's so crazy about his job, either. But it's probably embarrassing for him to have a mistake like that in his paper."

Kyan narrowed his eyes, studying her intently. "Why do you care so much if he's embarrassed?"

For someone who usually overflowed with self-confidence, Viv was looking uncannily timid. "I don't, I mean, not really." She shrugged, dropping her eyes. "But . . . I don't think it's fair to rip him apart. I've known lots of guys who are losers compared to him. That's all."

"I'm already writing up an apology for the next issue," I said bluntly. "That's more than enough."

What was going on today? First, Raj explodes, and now Viv was defending him?

I stood up, flustered and grumpier than ever. I wasn't sure I could take any more criticism, especially from friends who were supposed to be backing me up.

"I have to go back to the pressroom," I said, making a show of checking my watch. "I promised Raj I'd have that apology by the end of the day."

"Are you mad?" Viv blurted. "Please don't be mad. I'm sorry, I shouldn't have said anything."

"No, we're good." I smiled, but my muscles felt tight. The last thing I needed was weird tension with the only friends I had here, so I wanted to let this slide. "I'll talk to you later."

I gave them both a wave, then headed for the pressroom with a leaden heart, prepping myself for some serious humble pie.

My mood hadn't improved any by the time I got home from school that afternoon. The only saving grace of the day had been that Raj had been MIA from the pressroom when I'd written my apology, so I'd been able to leave it on his desk without facing any more of his lectures.

When I walked in the front door, the silence surprised me, and so did a smell that was as wonderful as it was familiar. Was I imagining it, or did I smell . . . Fenway Franks? Mmmmmm. My mouth watered as I walked into the kitchen. Destry and Gail were nowhere to be seen, but then I heard Dad's voice call from the family room, *"Anjinho*, is that you?"

"Dad?" I stared in astonishment at my dad standing in the middle of the family room in full Red Sox paraphernalia, foam finger, jersey, and all. "Um . . . what are you doing home?"

He grinned. "I took the afternoon off. And guess what we're going to watch?" He didn't wait for me to answer before announcing gleefully, "The 2004 win over the Cardinals!"

My heart leapt with excitement at the mere mention of that game. It was the game that had won the Sox their first World Series in eighty-six years. Sure, I'd only been three when it had happened, but that didn't matter. Dad and I had watched the game every year since then to commemorate the historic victory. It had been one of our traditions, way before Gail and Destry had entered the picture.

I sat down next to him as he started the game on the DVR, then glanced at the coffee table. It was stacked with all of my favorite Fenway snacks—Cracker Jacks, pretzels with mustard, and Fenway Franks.

"Wow," I said. "Did you do this?"

Dad nodded, handing me a hot dog. "Eat up. The smell of hot dogs makes Gail nauseous." He leaned toward me conspiratorially. "We have to get rid of all the evidence before she gets home."

"Definitely not a problem." I giggled, then took a big bite of my Fenway Frank.

As we ate, I forgot about my horrible day in the thrill of watching the game. I forgot about how complicated everything was with Dad and this new life. For a few hours, I stopped overthinking altogether. When that happened, being with Dad suddenly became easy and natural, like the way it had been before. We shrieked and hollered and clapped each time the Red Sox came an inning closer to their win. We spilled Cracker Jacks all over the floor, which I was convinced would freak Gail out, but only made Dad shrug, laughing. And when the final inning ended, we leapt off the couch, screaming and hugging each other.

"That game will never get old," I said afterward as we cleaned up the family room.

"Nope, and neither will watching it with you." He straightened to ruffle my hair. "You thought I forgot about it this year, didn't you?"

"No," I started softly, then stopped. We'd had such a great night. I didn't want to end it with a lie. "Well . . . maybe," I admitted.

"Lise," he said. "There may be a lot going on in this house right now, but I'll never forget about you. Not ever."

I smiled. "Thanks for remembering."

"Always," he said. "If the Red Sox could break the curse of the Great Bambino, I can certainly break this one."

"What do you mean?"

Dad popped a last bite of pretzel into his mouth, then sighed. "Blending families hasn't been as easy as Gail and I hoped it would be. That's all."

I gulped. "Dad, it's not my fault. I've been trying—"

"Hey, I'm not pointing fingers." He held up his hands. "There are four people in this house, and each of us has played roles in misunderstandings. I appreciate that you finished up the nursery by yourself. That was a step in the right direction." His eyes settled on mine in earnest. "Maybe, instead of trying just enough, we *all* need to try hard enough to make it work."

I stared at the ground, not sure whether the heat in my cheeks was from my usual frustration, or if it went deeper, heading toward shame.

Dad squeezed my shoulder. "Just . . . think about it, okay?"

I nodded. "I . . . I better do my homework." I started to turn away. It was the truth, but it was also an excuse to get out of the awkward conversation.

"Lise, one more thing," he called when I was halfway through the kitchen. His face was suddenly serious. "Gail and Destry and the new baby. They aren't *my* family. They're *ours*."

Ours. The word stuck in my head, beating out a guilty rhythm as I stared at my homework, trying to focus. When Destry came in to get ready for bed, I gave up entirely and headed for the family computer. I needed a reality check, and Simone could give those better than anyone else I knew. I wrote her a quick email:

```
To: SimoneMason@webmail.com
From: LiseSantos@webmail.com
Hey girl,
Miss you! It's late, and I'm thinking way too much.
Dad says I'm not trying hard enough with Gail
and Destry when I feel like all I do is try! What
if I'm not giving them a fair chance? Maybe the
problem is that I haven't been thinking of them as
family, even though (gulp) they kind of are. What
do you think? (Be brutally honest. I can take it.)
Newsflash: RAJ BATIK A CONFIRMED JERK. (Details when we
talk tomorrow.)
XOXO
Lise
```

I hit SEND and was about to log off when I saw a chat invite flashing in my FrogPrincess account. It was Raj. A wave of fresh anger heated my face, and my hand hovered hesitantly over the mouse. I could ignore him, or even end it tonight, right now, by telling him I was shutting down my account. But I was curious to see what was on his mind, to see if maybe I could finally unravel the Raj Batik mystery. I took a deep breath and opened the chat window.

RajBat:
Hey you. So glad you're still awake! Have you talked to Lise today?

I smirked at the screen. Little did he know.

FrogPrincess:
Of course. We're VERY close. She told me what happened.

RajBat:
She probably hates me. I came down on her pretty hard. Maybe too hard.

FrogPrincess:
Yeah. What was that all about?

RajBat:
I knew my dad would freak when he found out about the review. He doesn't like mistakes. But this was worse because it had to do with Principal Hinkle. Dad thinks I should've fact-checked Lise's review better, that I wasn't doing my job. It's so frustrating. Anyway, it's my baggage, but I sort of took it out on Lise.

FrogPrincess:
You could always try apologizing to her.

RajBat:
But then I'd be letting her off the hook. I trusted her to write truthfully, and she made a huge mistake.

FrogPrincess:
Yeah. She knows she messed up. It's just hard for her to admit it. She's going through some family stuff right now, too. Maybe cut her some slack?

RajBat:
Maybe. She'd be a lot easier to work with if she were more open-minded about her new job. She's not even giving it a chance.

Whoa. That was the second time I'd heard that in as many hours. First from Dad, and now from Raj. I was starting to take the hint. I swallowed down my pride and typed the next line slowly.

FrogPrincess:
She'll do better next time. Give HER that chance, ok?

RajBat:
Ok.

We chatted for a bit more after that, about movies, books, different things. Our tastes weren't always the same, but that only made it more exciting. Because even our debates over our differences were fun. Raj listened to my opinions and was never afraid to give his own. I felt like I could share anything with him, except who I really was. "Lise" never came up again, but I kept thinking about his "open-minded" comment.

We finally said good night, but I lay in bed for a long time afterward, replaying our conversation, and the one I'd had with Dad. I didn't need Simone to tell me what I already knew. All these weeks, I hadn't been giving Whitman, or my life here, a fair chance. Starting tomorrow, that was going to change.

Chapter Nine

"If I eat another bite, I'm going to be sick." Kyan gripped his stomach and stared at the mound of bite-size mini burgers in the center of the table. Given how skinny he was, I wasn't surprised. Where was he putting them all?

"Keep going," I said, ignoring my own growing heartburn. I grabbed an avocado-and-black-bean burger from the platter. "We have to taste them all."

I jotted down some notes on my ThinkPad. *Creamy, rich, with a pico de gallo bite.*

We'd been taste testing at Flare, the burger joint on Washington Lane, for the last two hours. I had notes on twenty different burgers I'd tasted so far today. That meant . . . "Only ten more to go," I offered brightly.

Kyan groaned. "Isn't there an easier way to make nice with Raj?"

"You know the answer to that," I said. "This review of Flare has to be perfect." I reached for the burger that had supposedly made Flare one of the top burger joints in New England. It was called the Independence Burger, and it was stacked with tomatoes, white onions, and—of all things—blue potato chips. (I guessed fitting in every patriotic color had been a stretch.) "I want Raj to see that I'm taking this job seriously. Even if it's not the one I wanted."

"You've been in the pressroom before and after school and during lunch every day this week. Trust me, he's getting the message."

"I'm not so sure," I said. Since Monday's disaster, I'd been putting in a lot of hours working on my two new assignments, but Raj had barely seemed to notice. He had muttered a two-syllable "Good work" when he'd skimmed my piece on Nino's Trattoria, but other than that, he spent his time in the pressroom darting from one person's desk to another, making grammar corrections, studying photo proofs, checking design layouts. He was never still for long, and I had the sense that he believed that was how it should be. "I've never seen anyone work so hard and look so miserable doing it."

"I have," Kyan said. "Viv."

My mouth dropped. "Viv? When?" I'd never seen Viv when she wasn't bubbling over with smiles and cheer.

Kyan shrugged. "I saw her doing a photo shoot at the mall once. She was sitting in a chair while this swarm of people flocked around her, fluffing her hair, smearing on layers of makeup. And her mom was harping on her the whole time, to smile this way, stand that way. Viv looked like a pill bug right before it curls up into its ball. Just . . . tired of being poked and pushed around."

"She's never told me about any of that," I said.

"No," Kyan said. "She doesn't make a big deal out of it, probably because most kids at school think her modeling gig is so cool. She doesn't want to come across as a whiner. But lately, she's been venting a lot to me. Sometimes she calls me at night, just to talk."

"Really?" I nudged him. "That's great!"

But Kyan looked doubtful. "We'll see. I'm not reading too much into it. I've been thinking I might actually have a shot with her if I was her token guy friend. You know, the shoulder to cry on after her next breakup." He shrugged. "I mean, why not? Underdogs get gorgeous girls in movies all the time, right? But she's so . . . flighty when it comes to guys." His eyebrows knit together. "Look, she's stringing Raj along like she likes him. She swears it's all part of the plan. But I'm not so sure."

My heart dipped, and I put down the rest of my burger, suddenly losing the rest of my appetite. "What do you mean?"

"I don't know exactly," Kyan said. "Maybe she's just stuck on the idea of actually having a nice boyfriend for a change. Sometimes I wonder if she really wants to fall for him. Not because they're right for each other. But because he's a decent option after a ton of bad ones."

"Well, she's allowed to be friends with him," I said, squirming uncomfortably. "It's good for her."

"Sure it is," he said forlornly. "We're both thrilled." He rolled his eyes. "Come on, Lise, you don't want her to be good friends with Raj any more than I do."

"Of course I do," I sputtered, feeling the blood rush to my cheeks. "Why wouldn't I?"

"Because. What guy *hasn't* crushed on Viv at some point? I bet

Raj is no exception. And you're scared he might fall for her for real. It's probably already happening." He pushed his leftovers around his plate dejectedly. "Are you still chatting with him online?"

I blushed. "Pretty much every night. Last night we talked for two hours straight." I smiled, remembering. "He emailed me a picture of a painting he's working on and asked me what it needed. I gave him a list of my favorite books, and he says he wants to read every one. We never run out of things to say. But then I come to school, and he gives me the cold shoulder. It seriously messes with my head."

"Well, that's because he doesn't know *you* . . . are you," Kyan pointed out.

I sighed. "True. When we chat, he's picturing Viv." I felt my mouth turning down at the corners. "But really, what does it matter if Viv's friends with Raj?" I asked, returning to the topic that was stressing me out. "She's got a list of potential Winter Formal dates that's a mile long. She showed it to us yesterday. And Raj isn't on it."

"Yet," Kyan challenged. "But every time they hang out, the odds go up. What if he asks her to the dance?"

My stomach bottomed out. How could that have never crossed my mind? "He won't," I said definitively. But I sounded a lot more confident than I felt.

"He might, and then what?" Kyan asked. "How could she say no to a guy who thinks she's a princess?"

I opened my mouth to argue, then shut it again. As much as I hated to admit it, he had a point. A good one.

As I walked home, my stomach ached, but I wasn't sure if it was from the burgers, or from what Kyan had said. When I'd come up with this plan, I'd been so sure it was foolproof. But what if Viv was starting to think of Raj as more than a friend? What then?

I tried to call Viv on her cell, but it went straight to voicemail. I knew she was missing school tomorrow for a photo shoot, but Friday was the field trip to Louisa May Alcott's house, so maybe we'd have a chance to talk then.

I pocketed my cell phone, my stomach tightening uncomfortably, and opened the door to our house. The second I stepped across the threshold, Destry's voice hit me square in the face.

"I don't know where they are, Mom," she was saying from the kitchen. "But don't blame me. I wouldn't have touched them with a ten-foot pole!"

"Well, pickled eggs don't just disappear!" That was Gail's voice, edgier than I'd ever heard it.

I thought about making an escape. I could probably go back outside without anyone noticing. But then I remembered Dad's words. *Our* family. For better *and* worse.

I shut the door, dropped my backpack and coat, and headed straight for the frontlines.

"Hey!" I called, walking into the kitchen wearing my cheeriest smile. "How's everybody doing?"

"Humph," said Destry, scowling.

Gail tried for a weary smile, without much success. "I'm looking for my jar of pickled eggs," she said to me. "You haven't seen them, have you?"

"No," I said, and then watched her face fall. "I'm sorry," I said quickly. "Um . . . maybe they're in the fridge?"

"We checked," grumbled Destry. "Five times." She heaved an enormous sigh. "Face it, Mom, you probably ate them and then forgot."

Gail lasered her eyes at Destry. "I *did not* eat an entire jar of eggs by myself!"

"Nobody else in this house ate them," Destry said, her voice rising to match Gail's. "The rest of us eat normal food."

I fought the urge to laugh. This may have been true, but now was definitely not the best time to point it out.

Gail straightened, pressing her hand against her back. "Well, then. Why don't the *normal* people in this house go to the store to get me more? *Destry?*"

"What?" Destry frowned. "You've got to be kidding! I just got home from ballet!"

"Yes, and you're still wearing your coat, which makes it easy." Gail handed her a ten dollar bill. "I'm going to take a nap." She waved as she left the kitchen.

"I cannot *believe* she's making *me* go," Destry seethed. "I have an Algebra test tomorrow, and I have so much studying to do . . ." Her voice wavered, and for a split second, her usually composed face faltered, and in its place was a softer, less guarded expression. It was like the curtain had suddenly been whisked back, and there was a stressed-out, ordinary girl behind it. How had I never seen her before? Maybe because Destry had been hiding her, or maybe because I hadn't *really* been looking.

Before I knew what I was doing, I blurted, "I'll go with you!"

We stared at each other, both in states of shock over the words that had come tumbling out of my mouth. I waited, wondering when the snarky remark would come. It never did.

"Um . . . okay," she said quietly. And then, an even more shocking, "Thanks."

I grabbed my own coat, and a few seconds later we were walking together down the street. I didn't say anything for the first block, thinking that as soon as I spoke again, the spell would be broken. But then, Destry shook her head and muttered, "Pickled eggs? Repulsive."

We looked at each other and burst out laughing.

"It's true," I gasped between hiccupping giggles. "And she probably *did* eat the whole jar. I saw her eat five in a row last night during dinner!"

We laughed so hard we had to stop in the middle of the sidewalk to catch our breath. Finally, once we could walk again, Destry said, "You know, part of me is dreading the baby coming, because it's going to change everything. But another part of me can't wait." She smiled. "Because at least Mom won't be a raving lunatic anymore."

"Don't bet on it," I teased, and then we were laughing all over again.

"So . . . I think I probably owe you an apology." Destry bit her lip, red with embarrassment. "I guess I've been a sort of wicked stepsister lately, haven't I?"

"Um . . . are you going to put a curse on me if I say yes?" I asked hesitantly.

"No." She laughed. "I knew I wasn't making it easy on you."

"You did?"

She nodded. "I've been kind of . . . jealous. Before you moved in, your dad was always bragging about you, telling Mom how great your grades were, and how proud he was of you being an editor-in-chief on the paper. I guess I was worried I'd never measure up to you."

I gaped at her. "Are you kidding? But . . . you're so beautiful! *And* popular! I don't get why—"

"I may be popular," she said, "but it's not the same as being a good student in your dad's book." She bit her lip, staring at the ground. "I bet you didn't know that I'm barely passing Algebra?"

"No," I said quietly. "Dad said you were struggling, but I didn't know how bad."

"Well, you do now. My real dad has never been that involved in my grades and stuff, so it's been tough having to listen to *your* dad, when my own is MIA half the time."

"I get that." I could tell from her beet-red cheeks that it was hard for her to be so honest, so I decided I owed it to her to bare all now, too. "And . . . I've been jealous of *you*." Now it was her turn to gawk, and it made me laugh. "It used to be that whenever I saw Dad, it was just the two of us. But since I moved here, I haven't spent that much one-on-one time with him." I smiled sheepishly. "I guess I'm not that used to sharing him yet."

"It's funny, I feel like that about sharing Mom with *you*. And it's only going to get harder when the baby comes," Destry said.

I nodded. "But it's exciting, too, don't you think? A new baby brother or sister?"

Destry wrinkled her nose. "That means dirty diapers."

"And babysitting," I added, wrinkling mine. "But maybe it won't be so bad if we work together."

"And *if* they pay us," Destry said. "I'll do the babysitting for free, but the diapers?"

I laughed. "That's definitely going to cost them."

We walked the last block to the store in comfortable silence and got two jars of pickled eggs. "Just to be safe," I told Destry. Then we headed for home.

"About your Algebra test," I said tentatively as we reached the front porch. "I can help you study, if you want." I waited, holding my breath, remembering what had happened the last time I'd offered to help her. This time, though, she gave me an open smile.

"That would be great." She leaned toward me, adding in a whisper, "Because if your dad uses the Red Sox in one more math equation, I'll scream."

"Not a problem. We can use shoes instead."

She grinned. "Now you're speaking my language."

We walked inside to a gushingly appreciative Gail, and when Dad got home, the four of us sat down to a dinner of easy conversation, talking about our days as if it were something we'd been doing forever. Gail and Dad swapped a few pleased smiles when Destry and I went to study together afterward. Then

Destry offered to let me use the computer first to write my review of Flare and send emails to Mom and Simone.

I wasn't sure if this new truce would last, but when I finally tiptoed past a sleeping Destry to go to bed, I saw twenty empty hangers and a generous chunk of newly cleaned out space on my side of the closet that hadn't been there before.

Thursday morning before class, I headed for the pressroom, ready to drop my review on Raj's desk. Because it was so early, I expected to find the room empty, but when I walked in, there was Raj bent over a table, a piece of charcoal in his hand, drawing. My heart instantly sped up at the sight of him with his sketchbook, his face intensely focused on the paper before him. I hadn't seen him looking like that since that night at Swoonful of Sugar, and it brought the memories brimming to the surface.

He didn't notice me at first, but then he suddenly looked up, smiling so genuinely that I was sure he was remembering that night, too. My breath caught in my throat as I waited, but a split second later, the smile dimmed.

"Hey," I blurted. "Sorry. I didn't mean to catch you by surprise."

"No, you didn't," he said, quickly slapping his sketchbook shut. "I mean, that was weird." He laughed softly to himself, shaking his head. "I thought you were Viv just now. The way you smiled reminded me of . . ."

"Who?" I was barely able to speak.

"Forget it." He turned away, starting to turn on the computers in the room to get ready for the staff to come in. "It's ridiculous. I mean, you don't look anything like her."

I forced a laugh while my insides wilted. A headline scrolled through my head: PRINCESS IS JUST AN ORDINARY FROG AFTER ALL. "No, I don't," I said softly. I felt his eyes questioning mine and quickly cleared my throat and pulled out my review, hoping to change the subject. "Here." I thrust it into his hands. "I finished the Flare review."

"Early, huh?" He nodded in approval. "That's a plus." I stood next to him and skimmed the words as he read them:

If your sizzle is getting frizzled by the same old boring burgers, it's time to give them some Flare. If you haven't visited this

Whitman fave lately, then you're missing out on some of the best burgers New England has to offer. With a recently expanded menu that includes vegan and gluten-free burger options, Flare has something for everyone to sink their teeth into. Of course, don't forget about their Independence Burger. One bite, and you'll be singing the praises of this star-spangled burger to all your friends and family. . . .

I swallowed, so nervous about what Raj's final verdict would be that I nearly jumped out of my skin when he laughed.

"Okay, I need you to translate," I said with a mixture of hope and trepidation. "Is that an I-like-it laugh or a you're-fired one?"

"I like it," he said, plunking it down onto the Approved pile of articles that were going to run in next week's issue. "It's really clever."

"Thanks," I said, feeling a strange pride in the work I'd done.

"Are you okay with it?" he asked. "I mean, with it not being one of those life-changing cover stories you used to write?" I was surprised that there wasn't an ounce of sarcasm in his voice. Only genuine curiosity.

I was as surprised as he was to find myself nodding. "I am. I'm still going to say that, honestly, it's not my favorite kind of writing. But . . . those are my words, and I had fun writing them." Then I decided to take a risk and motioned toward his sketchbook. "When I came in, you looked like you were having fun, too. I almost didn't recognize you."

He looked defensive until he saw my teasing smile, and then he cracked one of his own. "What? Don't I always look like I'm having fun?"

"Um . . . pretty much never," I joked. "When you're in the pressroom, at least."

I expected him to laugh, but instead, his face turned sheepish. "I was drawing. I guess I get lost in it sometimes, in the worlds I make on the paper."

"I could see that on your face before. You were in that other world."

He studied me, as if he was trying to come to a decision about something. Then he seemed to make up his mind, and added, "I . . . I've never said this out loud before, but I actually hate editing. I'd pick art over writing any day."

I stared at his face, watching the cloud descend over it again. "So why don't you, then?" I suggested, feeling brave. "You should sign up for a class with Mr. Diaz. He seems like a great art teacher. He already loves your work."

Raj frowned. "What? How does he know my work?"

Oh no! "Oh, he doesn't. I mean, I assume he *would* love it. You know?" *Whew, that was close.* "It's a hunch, that's all."

Raj looked thoughtful, but then shook his head. "It doesn't matter what he'd think. He's never going to see it. My dad would freak."

Well, now we were getting somewhere. "Because of the waste of time hang-up?" He looked as if he was about to ask how I knew, so I added a quick, "Viv told me."

"That, and because if I took art, I'd have less time to focus on the paper. If I'm on the law track, he doesn't want me distracted by 'fluff.' That's what he calls it." Raj sighed.

"You could try talking to him about it," I pressed. "If art makes you happy, then—"

"Then what?" He frowned at me. "I talk to Dad and, in an after-school special sort of way, he suddenly has a change of heart? That's not how he works."

"Okay," I said softly, not wanting grouchy Raj to return, when it seemed as though the two of us were finally connecting face-to-face for the first time since Swoonful. "Sorry."

His eyes softened. "No. *I'm* sorry." He gave me a small smile. "I should've known better than to bring up my dad. I get worked up every time. So . . . no more!" He smiled, then picked up his sketchpad. "Do you want to give it a try?"

"What . . . sketching?" I laughed, shaking my head.

"Oh, come on," he challenged. "I thought you were braver than that. Guess I was wrong."

I glared at him, sticking out my hand. "Give me that."

He grinned in satisfaction and set the sketchpad in my hands, along with a piece of charcoal. "We'll try something easy." He grabbed a tiny flower vase off one of the other editor's desks and set it on the table in front of me.

"What do I do first?" I asked, feeling suddenly self-conscious at trying my hand at something I knew so little about.

"Whatever you want," he said. "That's what's great about it. The freedom."

"Like writing," I said. "When I'm doing it for myself, and not as an assignment."

I stared uncertainly at the vase, then shooed Raj away. "I can't work while you're watching me. Go . . . slash some poor reporter's word count down or something."

"Funny," he said drily, but sat down across the room pretending to look busy with work.

I took a breath, then swept the charcoal in a slow curve across the page, trying to create the silhouette of the vase. I added another curve, and another, until slowly a shape started forming. I held the sketchpad at arm's length, then snorted. "It's all wrong. It looks like a deranged hippopotamus."

Raj came up behind me, surveying the page. "No . . ." he said judiciously, "it looks like a deranged hippopotamus *vase*."

I slapped him with the sketchpad, and he yowled playfully. Then he leaned toward me. "Let me show you," he said. He placed his hand over mine, slowly guiding the charcoal over the shape I'd made, rounding it out, adding in shadows. My hand warmed under his, fingers tingling at his touch. His chin hovered just above my shoulder, and his minty breath blew faintly across my neck in a way that made me dizzy. And then, our hands weren't moving on the page anymore. They were resting together, fingers entwined. It only lasted for a second before he pulled away suddenly, clearing his throat.

"There," he said awkwardly, without meeting my eyes. "That's better."

It wasn't better. It was . . . *heaven*.

"Um . . . I should get to class," I mumbled, standing up so quickly I nearly knocked the vase off the table. I righted it and handed him his sketchpad.

"Yeah, but . . . wait!" If it was possible for him to look even more bashful, he did. "There's something I wanted to talk to you about."

"Really? What?" I asked hopefully, then cursed myself for sounding so eager. I didn't want to end our conversation, but I didn't want to act like an idiot, either.

His cheeks deepened to a burnished walnut color, and he took a step toward me in a way that made my heart skip deliriously. Then he spoke.

"Viv."

"Viv?" I repeated faintly as my heart stopped, then fell with a *thump*. "Oh. Yeah. Viv. Right."

"I'm having trouble figuring her out. The first time I met her at Swoonful, talking to her was so . . . easy. But when I'm with her now, sometimes I don't know what to say. Online, we always connect. Like, amazingly. Over art, music . . . everything. But when we're together she seems sort of . . . bored by what I'm into."

"Well, what about stuff she's into?" I suggested, trying to keep calm. *You connect with* me *online!* I kept thinking.

"That's what I mean! We had this great chat about music online, but when I brought up Chopin yesterday, she said she hated classical music! How could she change her mind about that in less than twenty-four hours?"

"Oh," I said. Or, more like *uh-oh*. "Maybe she just . . . forgot?"

"About her taste in music?" he said. "Not likely. It's like, there's the girl I see at school, and then the girl in her IMs and emails." He shook his head. "She seems like two different people sometimes."

"Hmmm." I nodded, trying to look understanding while I smacked my internal forehead over and over again. Of course Viv seemed like two different people. She was! "Well . . . she *is* kind of shy."

Raj laughed. "No, that's not it. She's anything *but* shy." He paused. "I've seen other guys flirting with her in the halls. And sometimes, I feel like she's as into them as she is into me."

"But she's not," I said. *Yet,* I added mentally.

"You know what I mean though," he said. "She's beautiful and so confident."

"So that's why you like her?" I asked, my spirits sinking.

"Of course not. But she keeps every guy practiced in the art of drooling. I'd be an idiot to let her go. Right?"

I looked at him for a long time before saying quietly, "Who are you trying to convince?"

"No one!" he blurted. "I mean, *I* don't need convincing. I'm lucky she's interested in me at all." He paused. "I just wish we got along in person as well as we do online." He rubbed his forehead. "I know it doesn't make any sense—"

"It—it does," I stammered, my heart racing. "She feels the same way."

"Really?" His face brightened. "How do you know?"

I shrugged. "Oh . . . I just have a feeling," I said. Despite all the gushing he'd just done about Viv, I felt like I was in danger of melting into those eyes of his. What was wrong with me?

"I, um, I've gotta get to class," I managed to say.

He nodded reluctantly, and I could've imagined it, but I thought a trace of disappointment flashed across his face. "I'll see you tomorrow on the field trip?" he asked.

"Tomorrow," I said as I stumbled out the door.

So Raj acknowledged that we had a connection! Only . . . he thought it was a connection with Viv, not me. Only it was me, not her. But then he'd said Viv was beautiful, which was true. And that she was interested in him, which she wasn't. Only . . . what if she was? Now my head *and* my heart hurt.

I floated down the hallway in a daze, thinking about how much I wanted him to recognize me, how much I wished that he would somehow magically sense that I was the girl from that night. Not the Viv version of me, but the real, plain Jane, stubborn me.

As I sat down in English, trying to reorient myself to gravity, I realized what I had to do. It was time to tell him the truth.

Chapter Ten

I paced back and forth in front of the school, my impatient breaths puffing in the air like steam from a train.

"Where is she?" I grumbled. We were supposed to be boarding buses for our field trip to Concord in just a few minutes.

"That's the fourth time you've asked," Kyan said. "She'll be here."

I scanned the parking lot for Viv, but there was still no sign of her. I'd tried calling her again last night, but had only gotten her voicemail. She'd become friends with Raj, and everything had gotten so complicated. This was a delicate matter, and I felt like I needed to tell her about my decision face-to-face. And *before* Raj arrived.

Finally, I saw her mom's car pull up with Viv inside, frowning.

From the way they were talking and gesturing, it looked like they were having an argument. Viv finally got out and stalked toward us.

Kyan was at her side instantly, a look of concern on his face. "What's wrong?"

Viv threw up her hands. "Everything!" she cried. "I asked my mom if I could take a break from the modeling gigs, just for the spring. She completely flipped her lid."

"You want to give up modeling?" I asked. "Why?"

"Because . . . I don't even like it that much!" She scowled. "I'm tired of missing school to spend all day in some trailer while they paste my face with makeup. By the time they're done, I have more layers than a wedding cake!"

"But . . . I thought you loved getting the free clothes?" I said.

"I admit, that is a *huge* perk. Still, they're only clothes." She sighed. "I'm tired of everyone seeing me as a pretty face and that's it. I'm more than that, and I want to prove it." She gave a faint smile, shaking her head sadly.

Kyan pulled her into a sudden hug, which seemed to surprise him as much as it did her, because both of them pulled away awkwardly, blushing.

"It took some serious guts to even talk to your mom." Kyan cleared his throat, staring at the ground. "You should be proud."

"Thanks," Viv said, glancing up at him gratefully.

"Come on." I slipped my arm through Viv's as a line of buses pulled into the parking lot. Our teachers began drifting out of the school to start directing us to board. "We'll cheer you up on the bus ride."

Viv groaned. "I was so busy fighting with Mom, I completely forgot about the field trip!" She glanced down at her black ballet flats. "Raj said he wanted to walk with me up to Author's Ridge while we're there."

"He did?" I said hesitantly. Oh no. What if it was too late to tell Raj the truth about myself now?

"I think it's over a mile," Viv said. "I'll never make it in these shoes." She looked forlornly at the sturdy brown boots I had on.

Kyan nudged my arm, giving me a pointed look that I took to mean, "It's now or never."

I swallowed. This was my chance.

"Actually, Viv," I said, "I wanted to talk to you about Raj. I think . . ." I took a deep breath. "I think I want to tell him the truth."

Viv froze, her eyes widening as though I'd completely caught her off guard. "You do?" she said softly. "You do!" She smiled, but it seemed forced. "That's great, Lise! It's so much better to get everything out in the open."

"Really?" I said worriedly. "You're not upset? Because if . . . if you like Raj. As more than a friend, I mean. If you don't want me to—"

"Of course I want you to!" she said. "Why wouldn't I? Ben Jackson is going to ask me to Winter Formal any minute, and I've been racking my brain trying to figure out a way to let Raj down easy."

"You have?" Kyan narrowed his eyes doubtfully.

"This is perfect!" Viv went on brightly as we got in line to board the bus. "I'm not into hiking anyway, so *you* go on the walk with him and tell him then. And I'll . . ." Her voice faded, and she glanced around, looking lost.

"You'll hang out with me," Kyan said, looking proud of himself.

"Mom's put me in a foul mood," she warned. "I won't be good company."

"You're always good company," Kyan said simply, and Viv smiled at him.

"That would be great," she said. Suddenly, she raised her hand, waving. "Raj! Over here!"

I turned to see Raj walking toward us. My heart galloped at the thought of what I was about to do. As we climbed onto the bus, he barely said two words to me and Kyan, and my courage faltered. He had eyes only for Viv.

"I promised I'd sit with him on the bus," Viv whispered to me as we followed him down the aisle. "But once we get to Concord, he's all yours."

I nodded, but then they scooted into their seat and immediately began chatting in soft, for-your-ears-only tones. And I couldn't help wondering, *Is he really?*

"Are you sure you don't want to come on the hike?" Raj asked Viv as we stood in front of the antique house tucked away in its cozy, wooded enclave. We'd finished the walking tour of Orchard House, the home of Louise May Alcott and her family, and now the eighth graders were splitting up into several groups. There was a group that wanted to spend more time inside the house browsing through the museum, a second group that was heading to the Concord town center, and a third that was taking the walking trail to Sleepy Hollow Cemetery to check out Author's Ridge.

"My feet will never make it in these shoes," Viv said, but she said it a lot less cheerfully than she had earlier.

"But these are the graves of the greats," Raj insisted. "Louisa May Alcott, Ralph Waldo Emerson, Henry David Thoreau. People make pilgrimages to Concord just to see them!"

"I'm always getting Ralph and Henry confused." Viv crinkled her nose. "Which one wrote *The Scarlet Letter* again?"

"That was Nathaniel Hawthorne," I said, smiling and shaking my head at her. She may have been overdoing it, but I appreciated the effort she was putting into getting Raj on board so I could execute my plan.

"See?" Viv said. "I'm hopeless. I can't keep any of them straight. And you know what I think about seeing a bunch of dead authors' graves." She shivered.

"Oh." Raj looked more than disappointed.

Viv glanced at me, then gave Raj an encouraging smile. "Lise really wants to go, though. You guys are both into writing. I'm sure you'll have lots to talk about on the way."

"Okay," he finally said, but he looked at me with the same fallen expression someone would have being handed a consolation prize.

My hopes for the afternoon sagged. Maybe this wasn't a good idea after all. Kyan was the only one who seemed happy about this situation, and I knew it was because he'd get to spend the next hour or two with Viv.

"Have fun," Viv called cheerily. She looked worried as we turned down the street with the rest of our group, though, and I felt a stab of unexpected guilt. Then I checked myself. Viv had known all along that this was bound to happen, sooner or later. So why should I feel guilty?

Raj and I walked along the street in silence for the first few minutes. "It's beautiful here," he said.

"I know," I said, tilting my head back to look up through the trees. Their bare branches wove in and out of the dappled sunshine like a sprawling wilderness tapestry. "No wonder so many writers lived in this area. How could you not be inspired by this?"

"That's pretty much what Emerson said, too," Raj said, running his hands along the trunk of a birch tree. "'The good, the wise, and the great will have left their names and virtues on the trees.'" He smiled at me. "That's from the speech he gave at the dedication of the cemetery. I know it sounds strange, but I can almost feel them here. You know, in their words and ideas."

"That's not strange," I said softly. "I feel it, too. I think about that when I write, how I want to communicate ideas that matter to me." I picked a pinecone off the trail, turning it over in my hands. "That's why I fought you about the food beat. I wasn't trying to cop an attitude. I want to write about things I believe in."

"That's how art is for me," he said, his eyes lighting with enthusiasm. "When I'm starting a piece, I try to see the world in a new way. So that what I draw, you know, says something."

"How do you do it?" I asked. "See the world in a fresh way?"

"The world changes every second. It's just that most people get too bogged down in their routines to notice. Come on, I'll show you." He motioned for me to follow him off the path. As we broke through the tree line to a lookout point atop a rocky ledge, the sky and town stretched out below us in a beautiful landscape.

"Now . . . tell me what you see," he said. "Not the objects and their names. But colors, shapes, textures."

I studied everything—the tiny houses, clusters of bare trees, the bright wintery sky—imagining I was seeing them for the very first time ever. "Those trees over there." I pointed. "The way the light's hitting them makes them look . . . coppery. And those clouds look like feathers with icy pink tips." I laughed. "There's a light blue mist hanging over that valley down there. And . . ." I gasped in delight. "A red fox drinking from that creek!"

He grinned. "Wow, that's great, Lise. I didn't even see the fox." We stared out at the view for a few seconds in silence, and then he looked at me squarely. "Maybe you can do that same thing with your food beat. You know, think about giving your readers a fresh outlook on some place they've eaten at a dozen times already. Make them see it in a different way. That's way more challenging than just reporting on food."

"I've never thought about it that way," I said. "But . . . it makes sense."

He nodded. "And hey, you won't be on the food beat forever. I had to put you on it because that's where I needed you. But . . . you're a really good writer." I blushed at his compliment and thanked him. "If something opens up in Features or Op-Ed down the road, you'll be one of the top candidates," he added.

I raised an eyebrow. "*One* of the top?"

He elbowed me. "Now you're getting cocky."

"No way," I retaliated playfully. "You just can't handle the competition. Someday, I might be vying for *your* job, Mr. Editor-in-Chief."

"Believe me, I'd love it if you ousted me," he said with a laugh. "But who'd explain it to my dad?"

I scoffed. "Don't look at me. I've had enough Dad drama in the last month to last a lifetime."

"Really?"

I nodded. "Sometimes I think that parents try so hard to make kids happy that they have a tough time believing when they're not. But things with my dad are getting better because I was honest with him. Something *you* could try." I elbowed him back.

"You're relentless."

"And you're impossible," I countered.

He laughed, shaking his head. "We make quite a pair," he said, then instantly blushed. "I didn't mean, I meant—"

"It's okay," I blurted, giggling like a fool through my own mad blushing. "I know what you meant." But did I? Had that been a slip of the tongue, or something else? "We should, um, probably catch up to everyone else," I stammered, avoiding his eyes. I spun on my heel to head back to the path, but when I did, I lost my balance on the loose rocks under my feet.

Raj's hand caught my arm, and I felt myself melting at his touch. "Okay?" he asked softly.

No words would come, so I just nodded, trying to catch my breath and find my footing. He stayed close to me as we walked back through the trees, and I hoped fervently it was because he wanted to and not just because I was a klutz. In a few minutes, the path began to curve in and out of weathered, moss-covered headstones.

"We're here," I said quietly, stopping in front of the small headstone belonging to Louisa May Alcott. But we were alone.

"I guess the rest of the group must have walked ahead," Raj said. "Do you . . . want to catch up with them?" he asked, and I thought I heard some reluctance in his voice.

"Not yet," I said. "It's perfect this way."

"It is." He nodded, then reached into his messenger bag for his sketchbook. "I wanted to get some grave rubbings, and then sketch for a few minutes. If that's okay."

"Sure," I said. I left him to his sketchbook and went to do some exploring. Author's Ridge was a quiet, shaded spot with a lovely view of the gardens of the cemetery, sprinkled with the resting places of authors of ages past. I found the perfect rock a little ways away, lit with golden sunshine, and sat down on it to take it all in. I was thinking up an idea for a story when I felt a hand brush my shoulder. I opened my eyes to see Raj, his black curls lit with sun.

"It's probably time to get back," he said.

"Oh," I said sadly, not ready for the afternoon to be over. But Raj was already putting his sketchbook away. "Can I see what you were working on?" I asked.

He blushed. "It's . . . it's not finished yet," he said quickly. "Maybe some other time." He shut his messenger bag and reached out his hand to help me up off the rock. "Ready to go?"

I slid my hand into his and that instant electricity surged through my fingertips. I could have stood like that forever, but he let go, and I took a deep breath to calm my racing heart. It was now or never.

"Not yet," I blurted. "I, um, actually wanted to talk to you about something important."

"That's so funny," he said. "I was about to say the same thing."

"Really?" I squeaked, thinking I might hyperventilate. What was he about to tell me? That he'd figured out who I was? I clung to the hope as I watched his face, waiting.

"You first," he said, his eyes intent on mine.

"Okay." I could barely hear my own voice over the clanging of my pulse. "I guess what I want to say is, I'm not who you think I am." I gulped air. "I am, but . . . I'm not." He looked thoroughly confused now, and I shook my head. What, was I speaking in tongues? Why couldn't I just spit it out already? "What I mean is that I'm . . . I'm—"

"I'm sorry we got off on the wrong foot, too," Raj said.

The words *I'm the Frog Princess* died on my tongue. "Wait. What?"

"I'm sorry, too," he said amicably. "And I'm so glad we're becoming friends, because I feel like I can confide in you."

"About what?" I eked out. This did not sound good.

Raj blew out a breath of air, then announced, "I'm going to ask Viv to Winter Formal!"

I could've sworn that the world fell away as his words sunk in. But then I blinked, and I was still there, standing in the middle of a cemetery on a mild, sunshiny February day. I was alive. The world hadn't ended. The only thing bruised was my heart.

"W-wow," I managed to stammer. "But . . . I thought you weren't really connecting? You know, face-to-face."

Raj shrugged. "I figure we'll get there . . . eventually. If we're so good online, it's bound to roll over into real life sooner or later. There are probably a dozen guys planning to ask her to the dance. I don't want to risk losing my chance to be one of them."

"Right," I said, feeling numb. "That's . . . amazing."

Relief swept his face. "So you think she'll say yes, then?"

"I . . . I'm not sure," I said. Viv had told me a few hours ago that Raj was free for the taking. But now I remembered the stilted look on her face. And that unusually wide smile. How could I not have realized it before? That was her cover-girl smile, the one she wore when she was acting. And if Viv had been faking it, then that meant . . .

"I think she likes you." I swallowed, feeling like tweezers were pinching my chest.

"Really? That's great." He smiled. "At first, I actually thought she might be stringing me along. But that's not who she really is. The girl she is online is smart, funny. She's so beautiful, inside and out."

Beautiful. There was that word again. The one that had nothing to do with me, and everything to do with Viv.

"She's the girl I want to take to the dance," he finished.

Except that you don't know who she is! I wanted to yell. It was hard to look him in the eye, but I made myself. "So . . . you should do whatever your heart tells you to."

He grinned broadly. "Thanks. I will."

I was so quiet on our walk back to Orchard House that Raj asked me twice if I was okay. I answered that I was, but from his worried glances, I wasn't sure he believed me. Finally, I made up an excuse about having a headache and walked ahead of the rest of the group, leaving Raj chatting with his friends. All I wanted to do was get on the bus, try not to cry, and forget about everything that had happened.

Unfortunately, first I had to talk to Viv, and the sooner I got it over with the better. I found her and Kyan on a bench outside Orchard House, sharing the headphones on his iPod. Viv looked way happier than she had after her fight with her mom this morning. They looked so natural sitting there together, that if I hadn't known them, I would've mistaken them for a couple. But the instant they caught sight of me, Viv jumped to her feet.

"How'd it go?" Kyan asked. "Mission accomplished?"

"Mission aborted," I said. Before they could start with a million questions I wasn't in the mood to answer, I blurted, "He wants to ask Viv to the dance."

"What?" Viv gasped, her fair skin flushing scarlet. "But, but . . . how do you know?"

"He told me." I shrugged as nonchalantly as I could. "He really likes you."

"Me?" she whispered. A dreamy smile snuck onto her face, but then she quickly quenched it, looking worriedly at me. "Oh, Lise," she said. "How did this happen? I swear I didn't try to make him like me . . ."

"I know," I said, fighting down the lump in my throat. "It doesn't matter anyway. It's okay."

"No, it's not!" Kyan blurted, and I could see by his face that he was as crestfallen about this as I was. He turned to Viv, blustering. "You're—you're not going to go to the dance with him, are you?"

Viv bit her lip, looking more uncomfortable by the second.

"I think it depends on how you feel about him," I said to her. "Do you like him, too?"

I held my breath, waiting and watching as first confusion, and then guilt, swept over Viv's face.

"I . . . I don't know!" she cried. "I mean, this is totally unfair to you, Lise, but sometimes . . ." She put her head in her hands, and a muffled, "I think I might," squeaked out from between her fingers.

The world became a Tilt-A-Whirl again, but this time the dizziness didn't stop.

"Argh!" she cried. "I'm a horrible friend!" She frowned at me. "I'm sorry. It's just . . . I've never had a guy treat me the way he does."

"Hey!" Kyan protested.

She gave him an apologetic smile. "I meant a guy besides you," she said casually.

I was sure she didn't intend it to hurt, but suddenly the hopeful light in Kyan's eyes blinked out. Poor guy. I felt his pain.

"Who cares if there's no fireworks?" Viv continued, more to herself than to us. "The chemistry I had with all those other boys only ended badly. With Raj, there's something more. He's smart and interesting . . ."

"I know," I said softly. That was exactly the way I felt about him, too.

She looked at me guiltily. "Lise, I promise I won't go to the dance with him if you don't want me to. Just . . . tell me what to do."

She meant it. She'd do whatever I asked her to. The problem was, even though I wanted to change things, I couldn't. Viv deserved a shot with a nice guy. It should've been Kyan, but she was stuck on Raj. And Raj was stuck on Viv's beauty. So what was the point of all of us losing out on what we wanted?

Ignoring the ache in my chest, I finally said, "If you want to go to the dance with Raj, you should."

"But . . . what about you?" Viv asked. "You like him, too! You said so this morning."

"No, I didn't," I said carefully. "I said I wanted to tell him the truth." Ha! That was laughable, when I was lying right now. I took a deep breath. "I wasn't sure how I felt about him, either. But now I know." I shrugged. "Why would I want to be with someone who doesn't want me?"

I turned away, not sure how much longer I could last without giving myself away. "You know, I'm wiped after that long walk. I'm going to head for the buses."

"Me too," Kyan said quickly, following me.

"Oh, okay," Viv said, looking disappointed. "I guess I'll go find Raj, then." She looked at us hesitantly. "See you back on the bus in a bit?"

"Later," I said, waving and giving her my best attempt at a reassuring smile.

I hurried toward the buses with Kyan, trying not to think about how much I was dreading having to listen to Viv flirting with Raj on the way home.

"You okay?" I asked, elbowing him.

"Nope. You?"

"Not a chance," I said. "Got any audiobooks on your iPod we can listen to on the way back?"

He thought for a minute. "I uploaded *Romeo and Juliet* for English?"

"The story of a love at first sight doomed to end in tragedy." I nodded forlornly. "Perfect."

Chapter Eleven

The second I saw Viv waiting at my locker on Monday morning, I broke into a cold sweat. She was smiling hesitantly, but her eyes danced around mine without being able to meet them. I knew what it was before she even opened her mouth.

"So he asked you?" I said, more to get it over with than to make it easier for her. I knew I had no right to be irritated with her when I'd basically given her the green light already. But that didn't mean I wanted to think about it.

Viv nodded. "He called last night." Her cheeks took on a happy, rosy shine. She was glowing, no doubt about it. "And I said yes."

I mustered a smile even as my heart hit the floor. "That's great," I said quickly, focusing on swapping books out of my locker. "I'm happy for you."

"Really? Because I was scared to tell you." She took a shuddering breath. "I barely slept last night. I don't want things to be weird between us." She peered at me anxiously. "Are you sure you're okay with it?"

I glanced at her, feeling the truth on the tip of my tongue. But I couldn't bring myself to say it, seeing her standing there beaming with happiness.

"Yup," I blurted, praying that Kyan would show up so that I could be done with this conversation. We had a Bio quiz later today, and he'd told me he'd meet me here early so that we could review our notes. "Everything's fine."

Relief washed over her face, and she gave my hand an excited squeeze. "I'm so glad!" she squealed. "I was going to wear one of the dresses from my photo shoots, but then I decided I wanted something that *I* picked out myself. Will you go dress shopping with me? That would be so much fun!"

Oh, this was torture. "Sure," I said.

"It was weird when he asked me," she said, shaking her head. "I didn't even get butterflies. But I guess nice guys are sort of like brothers, right?"

"Um . . . brothers?" She lost me there. Kyan felt like a brother to me. But Raj? No way.

"Anyway, I don't need thrills." She giggled. "You know, I've had tons of crushes before, but this is different. This one's going to stick. I can feel it."

"It better," I blurted before I could stop myself.

Viv frowned in confusion. "What do you mean?"

Great. I had to go and say that out loud. I shut my locker and shouldered my bag. "I mean . . . I've heard you say the same thing about other guys before." So many times, and I hadn't even been in Whitman that long. "Just . . . don't dump Raj in a week, like you usually do, okay?" *Because I don't want him to get hurt, in spite of it all*, I thought.

Her frown deepened. "I don't *usually* do that." There was a defensive tone to her voice, but then her face brightened. "Besides, those other guys were jerks. I wouldn't do anything like that to Raj."

"Good," I said, and then thankfully, I saw Kyan waving from the other end of the hallway. "I've got to go," I said. "Kyan and I have a date."

"A date?" she repeated, her brow crinkling. "Wait, are you and Kyan . . . ?"

"It's a study date," I said. "You know I love Kyan, but not like that."

"Oh . . . right." Was it me, or did she look the slightest bit relieved? She giggled. "Kyan dating . . ." She shook her head. "I've never thought about that before. That would be sad."

"Why?" I said, feeling a sudden urge to defend Kyan. "Kyan's smart and fun! *And* cute."

"I know, Lise, I didn't mean *sad* as in *pathetic*. I meant *sad*, because if he had a girlfriend, then I wouldn't get to hang out with him as much."

I shrugged, clenching my teeth to stem my growing annoyance. "Well," I said, smiling as nonchalantly as I could as I turned down the hallway. "Nobody gets *everything* they want."

Viv waved, staring after me with a slightly puzzled look, and I felt a prick of guilt. Maybe it had been a little dig on my part, but I couldn't help myself. Did she expect every guy in this school to be at her beck and call?

My frustration must have showed on my face, because as soon as I reached Kyan, he asked, "It's official, isn't it?"

I nodded. "They're going together."

"I knew it." He sighed. "I've watched her go through boyfriend after boyfriend, but I've never been bothered this much before. I think it's because I'm worried this one might actually work."

"Me too," I said softly, shaking my head. "But . . . I guess we've got to get over it. Right?"

"How am I supposed to get over a crush I've had since pre-school?" He slumped down at one of the lab tables.

I thought about it for a minute. "By meeting someone else? Maybe at Winter Formal?"

He rolled his eyes. "Yeah, right. Nobody goes to that without a date."

I offered him an encouraging smile. "How about we go together?"

"You mean as friends?" he asked.

I shrugged. "Sure. Why not? It'll help me keep my mind off Raj, and your mind off Viv. Or, if it doesn't help, at least we can wallow in misery together."

Kyan laughed. "Thanks, Lise. If you were a bug, you'd be a tree lobster."

"Um . . . that's good I hope?"

He grinned. "It means you're the rarest, coolest ever."

"Ah." I slugged him playfully. "That's the strangest but best compliment anyone's ever given me. Thanks."

Even though I'd tried giving Kyan a boost of hope, I wasn't sure I'd actually succeeded. As for me, I felt beyond hopeless. Less like a tree lobster, and more like a squashed ant.

By the time I came home that afternoon, I was close to tears. The house was quiet, and there was a note on the kitchen table from Gail saying she'd gone to a doctor's appointment.

I grabbed a handful of candy from Gail's stash in the pantry, then headed upstairs to drown my sorrows in chocolate. I swung open the door and nearly slammed into Destry.

"Ouch!" she shrieked, grabbing one of her toes.

"Sorry!" I cried. "I didn't know you were right behind the door!" I sucked in a breath to prepare for her tirade, but she only waved her hand distractedly.

"I'm fine. I was trying to decide on this outfit." She motioned to the mirror hanging on the backside of the door. "But it looks horrible, like every other thing I've tried on." She flung herself onto the bed. "Ugh. I have nothing to wear!"

"Sounds like a disaster," I mumbled in a halfhearted attempt at a joke.

She lifted her head off her clothes to look at me. "It's not. Not really." Her eyes narrowed as she sat up. "But . . . *you* are! What's wrong? Your face is all scrunched and blotchy."

I bit my lip to keep it from trembling. "I've had a bad day."

"Is it my mom? Or your dad?"

"It's a boy," I muttered, not quite believing I was admitting that to her. But since our quest for pickled eggs, I was starting to feel as if Destry and I might actually—shocker—be bonding.

"I should've known. Disasters always involve boys." She groaned. "I've wasted two hours trying to figure out what to wear to Jake's birthday party, and it isn't until Friday."

"You *do* know it's only Monday," I said, and when she nodded, I added, "That's bad."

"Tell me about it," she said. "*And* . . . tell me about the boy."

I hesitated for a minute, but she looked so sincere—even sympathetic. Plus, I reasoned, she *was* a year older than I was.

That was a quantum leap when it came to boy expertise. So, I did what a few weeks ago I would've thought was impossible. I poured my heart out to my *not*-so-evil-stepsister.

"Whoa," Destry said when I'd finished telling her the whole saga. She held out her hand. "Give me some chocolate. Even *I* need some after hearing that."

I laughed, handing her a piece. "What do you think?"

"Well, aside from Viv trespassing on your territory, which she totally did—"

"Unintentionally," I added in Viv's defense. (Although it was nice to feel validated, I had to admit.)

"Whatever," Destry said, as if the point wasn't even debatable. "You." She jabbed her finger at me. "Need to tell Raj everything. How can you expect him to know what he's doing when he doesn't even know who he likes?"

"He likes Viv." I stuffed another piece of chocolate into my mouth. "It's too late to tell him now, especially when this whole thing is my fault to begin with. Besides, I couldn't do that to Viv."

"But you're forgetting one really important thing," Destry said. "Raj is falling for the wrong girl. He thinks Viv is *you*."

As annoying as her condescending, big sisterly tone was, she had a point.

Still, I told her, "It doesn't matter what he thinks. What he sees in Viv is someone gorgeous and popular and . . . perfect. Everything I'm not. And . . . that's the girl he likes. He told me himself."

"I'm not buying it," Destry said. "I don't think you're giving Raj enough credit. He doesn't seem that shallow. Besides, you're a lot prettier than you seem to think you are."

"Thanks." I smiled, knowing Destry wasn't the type to just hand out compliments. "And thanks for the advice. I'll think about it."

"Anytime." Destry nodded. "But better think fast. The dance is this Saturday." She stood up. "Now, it's your turn to give *me* some advice." She sighed at the mountain of clothes on her bed. "Help me figure out what to wear so I have somewhere to sleep tonight?"

I raised my eyebrows. "You're asking *me* for fashion advice?"

"Hey," she smiled sheepishly, "isn't that what sisters are supposed to do? *But* . . . I have veto rights."

I giggled. "You got it."

By the time Gail and Dad came home from the doctor's, Destry and I had solved her crisis, but I wasn't any closer to solving mine. Wardrobe dilemmas, as it turned out, were much easier to figure out than boys.

I sat through dinner exhibiting the social skills of a zombie, but only Destry, who shot me sympathetic glances across the broccoli every few minutes, knew what was wrong. As much as it pained me to think about Raj, it was also fun, in a weird way, sharing a secret with Destry.

"What's going on with you two?" Dad asked at one point.

We just shrugged, gave each other conspiring glances, and ducked our heads over our dinner plates. Dad finally gave up and cleared the dishes while Destry and I hunkered down in front of the TV with a bowl of popcorn. After all the studying we'd done together, Destry had gotten a B on the Algebra test she took last week, so Dad and Gail were willing to let the "No TV on school nights" rule slip, just this once.

It was an ordinary, nothing special sort of night—a comfy sweatpants and ponytails night—exactly the sort of night I would've had with Simone in Boston. But it was nice to have Destry beside me, munching popcorn, giggling, and chatting with me. It felt . . . normal, the way my life had felt normal back at Mom's.

When I went to sleep that night, though, I was restless again. My mind ticked off every practical reason for letting Raj go, but my heart wasn't in a listening mood. When I finally drifted off, my dreams were filled with visions of Raj, smiling at me in the candlelight at Swoonful of Sugar, lifting a sweet macaron to my lips.

Chapter
Twelve

"Earth to Lise." A hand flashed in front of my face. "Come in, Lise."

I blinked, and there was Viv, standing in the dressing room before me, wearing another impossibly perfect dress.

"Sorry," I said. "I was just thinking about the review I'm working on."

"Right. Like you were just thinking about your English paper five minutes ago, and your Algebra quiz five minutes before that." Viv arched her eyebrow. "What's up with you today? You're supposed to be helping me decide on a dress, and instead, you're orbiting space."

I forced a laugh, but laughing was the last thing I felt like doing. I'd been at the mall with Viv for hours, watching her try on dress after dress, getting more impatient and crabby by the second. I'd agreed to go shopping with her, wanting to prove that I could be a mature, supportive friend, no matter how I felt about Raj. But I hadn't banked on the fact that she was going to gush over Raj so much this week, and worse, that she actually knew next to nothing about who he really was. She admitted she was getting tired of his "art talk," but in the next breath told me how amazing it was that he held doors open for her.

"I'm sure we have other things in common," she reasoned. "I have to figure them out, that's all."

I couldn't stand it, and it was only Wednesday. How was I going to survive the three more days until the dance?

"You look fantastic in everything you've tried on," I said, which was true. Viv would've looked fantastic wearing a burlap sack. "Maybe you should just . . . pick one?"

"I can't!" Viv eyed her current dress in the mirror, then flipped through all the others she'd already tried. "I want Raj to think it's perfect. How do I know which one he'll like?"

Ugh. This was like a Viv version of the conversations I'd been having with Raj in the pressroom all week. Every day, he started in on me with a new set of questions. Should he give Viv flowers before the dance? What was her favorite flower? Where should he take her to eat beforehand? Each question chipped a little further into my armor, and each day I felt more exposed, and less certain I'd be able to keep acting like everything was okay.

Now, I skimmed the dresses hanging on the rack, thinking of Raj's paintings. They were so full of bright colors. I was sure he'd like the candy-pink dress Viv had tried on a few minutes before. But I couldn't bring myself to say it.

"You know Raj better than I do," I said to Viv. "What colors would he like the best?"

I was being horrible, testing her this way just to try to make myself feel better. But even as I scolded myself, I felt a shameful satisfaction in watching Viv struggle with the question.

"Um . . . I'm not sure," she said, looking stressed. "We've never talked about that." A worry line formed on her forehead, but then she shook it off, smiling. "But I really feel like we understand each other without having to talk much, you know?"

Oh, please. I resisted the urge to roll my eyes. I needed to get out of here, before I lost it. "He likes bright colors," I finally said. "Get the pink dress."

"Great! Thanks!" she said, setting it aside and stepping back behind her dressing room door to change into her regular clothes. "So," she said, her voice muffled under the clothes she was pulling on, "I can't believe you and Kyan are going to the dance together."

"Why not?" I said, bristling. "Friends do things like that all the time. Don't read into it, okay? Kyan's not the one for me."

"No, I know," she said. "You're not his type at all."

"Really?" I flushed, gripping the sides of the bench. "I'm not Raj's type, either, I guess. Maybe I'm not anyone's."

"Oh, Lise," Viv said softly, sticking her head around the dressing room door. "That came out wrong. That's not what I meant."

I sighed. "I know. So . . . who *is* Kyan's type?"

"I—I—" Viv stammered. "I don't know. It's just . . . weird to think about at all. I had no idea he even wanted to go to the dance."

"You don't sound happy about it," I said.

"No, it's fine," she said quickly. "I want him to be happy."

I shrugged. "I'm only going to cheer him up." I stood up, wanting this conversation to be over. "He actually wanted to go with someone else, but she's always spoken for."

"Really?" Viv asked, slipping on her cardigan over her shirt. "Who?"

I shrugged. "It doesn't matter. It was never going to happen."

"Why didn't he tell me about her?" she asked. "He tells me everything."

"He didn't have to," I said. "It was pretty obvious. I guess just not to you."

"Huh," Viv said, then gave me a puzzled glance as I turned toward the door. "Wait . . . where are you going? Aren't you going to try on some dresses, too?"

"Nah, not right now." I shrugged. I'd thought maybe I'd find a dress for myself tonight, but now I wasn't in the mood. I knew Raj was going to be blown away by Viv at the dance, and trying on anything with Viv in the same room felt impossible.

"Just try on a few, please?" Viv emerged and grabbed my arm, playfully pulling me toward a dressing room. "Kyan's favorite color is red, and you'd look fab in red."

"We're going as friends, remember?" I said. "And anyway, I, um, already know what I'm wearing." That wasn't true, but it was the best explanation I could think of. I started for the exit. "I'll meet you by the registers."

"Okay," she said, sounding disappointed.

She came out a few minutes later, holding a cherry-red floor-length chiffon number.

"What happened to pink?" I asked.

Viv shrugged, blushing slightly. "Oh, you know, red's more my color."

I stared at the dress as she draped it over the sales counter, irritation simmering in my veins. What was she trying to do, mess with Kyan's head, too?

Maybe she didn't have any motives. After all, she didn't have a clue Kyan liked her. Maybe the red dress was her favorite, and it was as simple as that. But still, it didn't seem fair.

After she paid for the dress, we walked to the food court for ice cream cones, but I barely tasted mine, eating it mechanically as I listened to Viv debate with herself over how to wear her hair to the dance.

"What do you think?" she asked. "Up or down? Kyan told me once that he liked it when I wore my hair up, but Raj has never told me what he likes."

"It looks okay either way," I said flatly.

"Okay?" Viv repeated worriedly. "But I want it to look great! I mean, if I wear it down and then he tries to kiss me, it might get in the way, but then if it's up and glued to my head with hairspray, he won't want to touch it."

"Just fix it however you want!" I said, exasperation creeping into my voice.

"Yeesh, okay." Viv stared at me from over the top of her ice cream. "Hey, are you mad or something? You seem pretty tense—"

"I'm fine," I said, way too quickly. I checked the time on my phone. "I . . . I forgot that Gail said she'd be here at six. I've got to go." I nearly dropped my ice cream cone in my hurry to grab my purse.

"You didn't tell me that before—" Viv started, perplexed, but I was already waving, calling over my shoulder that I'd see her at school tomorrow.

Five minutes later, I was standing outside the mall's main entrance, freezing as I dialed Gail's cell. She sounded surprised when I told her I was done shopping already. I'd originally told her to pick me up at eight, but she said she'd come get me, no problem. I sighed as I hung up the phone. I'd have to wait another fifteen minutes in the frigid air, but I'd much rather shiver than talk to Viv about her plans to kiss *my* dream guy. It wasn't lying, I reasoned. It was self-preservation, and I'd do it for as long as it took me to get over Raj.

Getting over Raj would've been much easier if I didn't have to see him every day. But not only did I have to see him; I had to work with him. And listen to him talk about how much he was looking forward to the dance. It was torture, and by Friday after school I felt strung so tight that I worried the slightest little hiccup would make me snap.

Then . . . the hiccup happened.

I was watching Raj's face as he read my new review on Wild Bamboo, the vegan restaurant on the outskirts of town. He was sitting so close to me that our elbows were grazing, and I was trying to hold my breath, because his clean, fresh smell was driving me to distraction. Finally, he looked up, shaking his head.

"What happened here, Lise?" he said quietly, sliding the review across the desk to me. "This isn't your best work. Not even close."

"What do you mean?" I asked as my stomach lurched. But even as I asked, I knew the answer. The review had taken me twice as long to write as my earlier ones, but was only half the length. As much as I'd tried to infuse it with enthusiasm, every word had fallen flat on the page. *Raj, Raj, Raj* was pounding in my head even as I'd pounded the keyboard, and I couldn't shake it.

With my nerves quaking, I reread the first few lines of the review: *Wild Bamboo sits on the edge of town and plays host to a variety of culinary appetites. It offers everything from cauliflower tempura to tofu sausage. Even non-vegan diners will delight in the menu. . . .*

I dropped my eyes, not able to read anymore. It was so . . . so utterly boring, and I had no defense. Except that it was all *his* fault! Of course, I couldn't say that, so I blustered, "I don't know what the problem is. I think it's fine."

"No way. You're too good a writer to be letting yourself off the hook for subpar work. It would be great if you could fix it ASAP, because I've got another piece I want you to do for the weekend.

You're going to cover the grand opening of Swoonful of Sugar this Sunday."

Swoonful of Sugar.

I felt my throat closing in panic. No way. I couldn't. It would be too hard, remembering everything that had happened there with him that would never happen again.

"No," I blurted. "I . . . I won't do it."

Raj threw up his hands in frustration. "Come on, Lise, don't tell me you're protesting the food beat again? I thought we were done with that—"

"It's not that," I said softly. "I just can't."

"You can't." He stared at me, then blew out a breath, folding his arms across his chest. "Why not?"

I shook my head, blushing, then finally mumbled, "I can't tell you."

"Fantastic." He snorted. "Well, here's what *I* can tell you. You fix the Bamboo piece and do the Swoonful review, or you lose your job."

"What?" I stared at him in disbelief. "You can't be serious!"

"Well, what am I supposed to do?" he cried. He sat back in exasperation, then looked at me long and hard, and his expression softened. "Lise, what's going on?" he asked gently, leaning forward. "You've been acting strange ever since the trip to Concord, and I don't get it. I thought we were friends." I cringed at the idea that I was hurting his feelings without him understanding why. "Now you only talk to me when you have to, and you have this attitude when you're here at work. I know something's wrong . . ."

My pulse skyrocketed, and I felt as if my soul was bared in mortifying glory right there on my blazing face. "Everything's f-fine," I stammered.

He shook his head. "But you're refusing to write the Swoonful review, and there's none of you in that Bamboo review, either. It's like your heart wasn't in it."

I glared at him, frustration an exploding firecracker in my brain. I snatched up the review and whipped away from him. "You're one to talk about hearts," I snapped, loud enough that several kids lifted their heads from their computer screens. Raj gave them warning glances, and immediately the heads bent down again. "Where's yours?" I demanded. "Not in this pressroom, that's for sure."

"What are you talking about?" he said as he led me into the hallway.

I scowled at him. "You're playing this editor-in-chief power trip because you don't have the guts to tell your dad about your art."

"You know why I can't tell him," he said through clenched teeth. "He doesn't understand. He'd only make me stop."

"You haven't even tried talking to him, so you can't possibly know how he'll react. Instead, you spend all your time running the pressroom like some dictator."

"I'm doing my job," he said gruffly.

"A job you don't even like!" I stabbed a finger toward the pressroom. "Nothing you do here is you. It's just who your *dad* wants you to be! How can you even know who you want when you don't know who you are?"

"*Who* I want?" He frowned in confusion.

My heart froze. Oh no. I did *not* just say that. "I meant *what*. What you want." I shook my head, avoiding his gaze.

He took a step toward me, his eyes intense on my face. "But you said *who*—"

"Forget it!" I cried, turning away in panic. "Just . . . go hide in the pressroom! You're good at that! But don't you dare tell me what's wrong with my writing. I don't want to hear it. Not from you." I glared at him fiercely. "And you don't have to fire me. I quit!"

I turned on my heel and plunged down the hallway blindly, feeling tears threatening. I thought I heard my name being called, but I didn't look back, and I didn't think he'd follow me. Not after I'd said all those horrible things to him. There was my name again, and this time it was louder. I ran faster, and then suddenly, slammed into someone who immediately grabbed my hands.

"Let me go, Raj!" I blurted, but when I opened my eyes, Viv was the one holding onto me.

"Raj?" she repeated softly, confused. "I was on my way to say hi to him." She leaned closer. "Hey, are you . . . about to cry? What's going on?"

I sucked in a ragged breath. "We had a huge blowup over a stupid article! I just . . . lost it!"

Viv folded her arms. "So you took it out on him. I get it." She frowned. "You've been like that with me, too, biting my head off all week."

"I have not!" I blurted, even though I knew it was true.

"This is about the dance, isn't it?" Viv said. "You've been out of sorts ever since Raj asked me to go with him. You barely said two words about the dresses I tried on the other night."

I wanted to cover my ears, to deny everything. But I couldn't. Not anymore. "Fine! Yes, it's about the dance!" I hollered. "I don't want you to go with Raj!"

"What?" Viv gasped.

"I told you I was okay with it, but I'm not! I . . . I still like him, even after everything. Even though you do, too. I know it's not fair, but . . . I can't help it."

I watched as Viv's face transformed, from hurt into fury. "I can't believe you're telling me this now! The dance is tomorrow night!" she cried. "You should've been honest with me from the start."

"I know," I muttered. "I—"

"What do you expect me to do? Give him up?" She shook her head. "You can't change your mind about him on some whim."

"Oh, come on, Viv! Don't talk to me about whims!" I cried. "You have more crushes than celebrities do! It's like a game to you. Your crush on Raj isn't real."

"That's not true," she started, her face paling. "I'm just trying to find my perfect guy. He *could* be Raj."

"He's not." I rolled my eyes. "You never needed to find the perfect guy. He's been there for you this whole time, only you don't see it! And Raj is *not* him."

Viv sniffed. "I don't know who you're talking about, and you don't know the first thing about how I feel about Raj," she snapped. "I'm *going* to the dance with him."

"Then you're going with the wrong guy," I said as my lip quivered. "And I'm not going at all."

I rushed past her and slammed through the school doors as the tears I'd been holding back finally began to fall.

● ● ● ● ●

I've never been so thankful for winter in my life as I was when it started to snow in fluffy, cascading sheets. I passed crowds of kids leaving school, but their heads were bent under their hats. So, no one noticed my tears.

When I got home, I headed straight upstairs and threw myself on my bed, getting ready to give my pillow a thorough soaking.

I didn't get far, though, because soon there was a knock on the door.

"Please . . . go away," I mumbled into my pillow.

The door swung open and Destry's voice said, "No can do. It's my room, too, remember?" The bed dipped to one side as she sat down beside me, but I didn't lift my head. "I know what happened," she said softly. "I brought some reinforcements."

I sniffled and wiped my eyes, reluctantly raising them to see Kyan standing at the foot of the bed. "What's this I hear about you backing out on me?"

"How did you find out?" I said as Destry handed me a tissue. I glanced at her. "And how did *you*?"

"I went to Becca's house after ballet," Destry explained. "I was there when Viv called Kyan."

"Great," I muttered, looking at Kyan. "So she told you about my meltdown. What did she say, that I was trying to steal Raj away from her?"

"No," Kyan said. "She was upset, but she didn't sound that angry. She asked if I'd still come to the dance if you didn't. She said she was nervous and wanted me to be there."

"She wants *you* there, and Raj, too?" I rolled my eyes. "Why should she get everything she wants? And how can you stand being around her when you know she'll never like you?"

He shrugged. "I guess I don't think in nevers. More in maybes. Besides, I don't want to lose her as a friend." He sat down next to me. "But it's not easy for me, and the deal was we were supposed to do this together, remember?"

I sighed. "I can't go. I don't want to see them together."

Kyan glared at me. "And you think I do?"

"Um . . ." I plucked at the bedspread. I knew he was right.

"Lise," Destry said. "The best way to get over Raj is to go and have a great time. Prove that you can be around him without falling apart."

I flopped back on the bed. "I don't know. I never even bought a dress, and I don't have anything to wear."

Destry jumped up. "I can fix that!" she said, hurrying to the closet. She held up a shimmering teal strapless sheath, and I caught my breath. It was the dress I'd wanted to wear to the Valentine's party, but she hadn't let me. I took it as a promising sign of how much our relationship had grown.

"It's beautiful," I said, carefully taking the dress from her hands. "Thank you."

Kyan smiled hopefully. "Does this mean you're going to the dance?"

I hesitated, but then took one more look at Kyan's pleading eyes and caved. "Okay. I'll go."

After all, it was only one night. I could survive one night. Right?

Chapter
Thirteen

"I'm not going to survive," I said, pulling my coat tighter around me. A dozen kids brushed past, disappearing into the purplish glow and pumping music that flowed out through the open gym doors.

"Yes, you will," Kyan said. "Look at me. I'm fine."

I gave him a "yeah right" glance. "You tried on ten different neckties before we came, *and* you dropped your mom's camera into the kitchen sink."

We'd gone to Kyan's house before the dance for pictures, and Mrs. Slade had promised to take some for my dad and Gail, who'd had to stay home because Gail's back was killing her. Dad had told me he was sorry he couldn't bring us to the dance himself, but he was on "baby watch," as he called it. According to Gail's doctor, the baby could come any time now, and Dad wanted to stay close by.

"Well, I'm fine *now*," Kyan said huffily. "All I needed was my lucky scarab tie, and I'm dauntless. Bring it on, I can take it." As far as bug ties go, the burgundy-and-gold scarab tie was actually very cool. I was sure he was making the Science Club proud.

I grinned at him. "Hmmm, maybe we should just stick to the snack table?"

He shrugged, laughing. "Ready?"

"As I'll ever be." I straightened my shoulders, took a deep breath, and walked into the dance hall. The gym had been transformed into a winter wonderland, complete with glittering white and purple lights, and silver snowflakes and tinsel streaming from the ceiling. A crowd of couples were already on the dance floor, and my eyes automatically swept over them, looking for Raj and Viv. I didn't see them anywhere.

"I don't see them, either," Kyan said, reading my thoughts as he took my coat. "I'll go check your coat and be right back."

I nodded and made a beeline for the snack table (aka the shy people's safety zone). As I grabbed a cup of punch, I felt a tap on my shoulder. I whirled, expecting Kyan, but my heart stopped at the sight of Raj in a sleek navy suit, his curly locks combed back from his forehead. He looked dashing and brooding and . . . dreamy.

"I thought it was you," he said, running a hand through his hair self-consciously. "Viv said you weren't coming tonight. But I'm glad you did. You look . . . incredible." As he said that word, he blushed and I could feel my own face turn hot. Why would he say that? Did he mean it? Destry had helped me with makeup before the dance, and I did have to admit that when I'd glanced into the bathroom mirror, I looked pretty nice.

"Thanks," I finally said, trying to sound calm. I glanced around, dreading the awkwardness that was sure to follow the second Viv arrived. "Where is Viv?"

"Oh, she's in the bathroom with Mona and some of the other girls." He shrugged. "I guess they're doing touch-ups for photos."

A slow love song came on, and the lights dimmed as couples took the floor. I felt Raj's eyes on my face, and my heart drummed louder than the bass from the speakers.

"Would you like to dance?" he asked softly.

A disbelieving laugh popped out of me. "You're kidding," I said. "Aren't you mad at me? I quit the paper yesterday."

"You didn't," Raj said firmly. "Because I refuse to accept your resignation."

I eyed him doubtfully. "Is that so?"

He nodded. "See, I have this theory about you." He leaned toward me, his lips nearly brushing my ear. "You don't really want to quit," he whispered.

"I don't?" I said breathlessly.

"No," he said decisively. "And when you're ready to tell me what's going on, you'll turn in your reviews." He shrugged. "I can wait, and in the meantime, we can dance."

"I . . . I . . ." I wanted to. So much. I couldn't even be mad at him anymore. I couldn't be anything, except completely and hopelessly in like. "Thanks, but . . . I don't think I should. I'm waiting for Kyan, and Viv will be back any minute." I looked around anxiously, hoping to spot Kyan coming to my rescue.

"Viv won't mind if I share a dance with a friend," Raj said. "Come on." Before I could protest again, he took my hand, gently pulling me toward the dance floor. When he slipped a hand around my waist, I thought I would melt into a puddle.

"Why are you being so nice to me anyway?" I asked. "You should hate me after losing it with you yesterday—"

"No!" he interrupted. "No. What you said about my dad and . . . everything else. You gave me a lot to think about." His eyes met mine with an earnestness I hadn't been expecting. "Yesterday after you left, I talked to Mr. Diaz, the art teacher. I showed him some of my paintings, and he wants to showcase them in the art show in a few weeks."

"Oh my god," I said. "That's great!"

Raj nodded, a hesitant smile crossing his face. "It will be . . . *if* I tell my dad." He frowned. "I haven't decided what to do yet."

"If you'd let him see your art, I'm sure your dad would come around."

"I wish I had your confidence."

I snorted. "I'm not always confident, trust me. Especially when it comes to admitting mistakes." I smiled. "You *were* right about my review. I was just too stubborn to admit it."

He nodded, then stepped closer. "You are stubborn, but so am I. I'm sorry we fought." He laughed softly, shaking his head. "Something about you brings it out in me."

I smiled. "I know the feeling."

Raj studied me with his bright green eyes and I felt my temperature rise. "Lise," he whispered, "this is going to sound crazy, but sometimes I wonder if—"

If what? I thought, my mind spinning with hopeful possibilities. But I didn't get the chance to find out, because a second later Viv was at his side, giving me an aloof, slight smile.

"Here you are," she said to him, then to me, added an emotionless, "Hey."

"Hey," I said softly. Viv looked even better in the red dress tonight than she had at the mall. Raj couldn't seem to take his eyes off her.

Viv laughed tensely. "I didn't expect to see you two on the dance floor."

Raj dropped his eyes. "Lise was, um, keeping me company while I waited for you."

"Sure, no biggie." Viv nodded, but there was a tightness on her face, like she was trying too hard to look happy. "Kyan's looking for you," she said to me. "He's at the snack table."

"Okay," I said, wondering what kind of shape Kyan would be in after seeing Viv. I doubted even the scarab tie could conquer a knockout red dress.

Viv straightened the collar of Raj's jacket. "It's picture time!" she said cheerfully.

Raj lifted his hand to me in a stilted wave. "See you later?"

I nodded as they walked away. Then, with sinking heart, I went in search of Kyan. He wasn't at the snack table, though, and finally I spotted him motioning frantically from the exit, my coat in his arms.

"Oh, Kyan, I'm sorry," I said when I reached him. "It was Viv's dress, wasn't it? If you want to call it a night, that's fine."

"Forget Viv's dress," he said. "It's the baby! My mom called my cell. She's outside with Destry. She's going to drive you to the hospital. Gail's in labor."

"Omigod!" I shrieked, grabbing my coat from him, my adrenaline surging as I raced for the door. It took me a second to realize Kyan wasn't beside me. I turned back to him. "Aren't you coming?"

Kyan shook his head. "Mom'll come back for me later." He smiled. "I promised myself I'd dance with Viv tonight. Just once, no matter what. I know she's spoken for, but . . . I'm doing this for me. I'll regret it if I don't, because after tonight, I'm letting her go."

I grinned at him, then ran back to give him a hug. "She'll never know what she missed out on," I said.

"Thanks," he said as I turned to go. "Call me as soon as you can with news!"

I waved, then hurried out, jogging down the sidewalk in a rush of excitement.

But as I rounded the corner to the parking lot, I caught sight of the outdoor gazebo on the school lawn and stopped dead. Standing under the gazebo's garlanded dome were two figures, heads bent together, silhouetted against the starlight. One of them was wearing an unmistakable red dress.

It was Viv and Raj. I sucked in a breath as I watched their heads tilt together, lips moving closer . . . I clenched my eyes shut, my heart aching, not wanting to see the kiss. Then I double-timed it to Mrs. Slade's minivan, without looking back. I climbed into the back beside Destry, sinking down into the seat with a heavy sigh.

"Can you believe Mom's having the baby?" Destry cried. "How was the dance? Did everyone love your dress?" Then she took one look at my face and gasped. "What's wrong?"

"I saw them kissing," I said quietly. "It's over."

"Are you sure they were kissing?" Destry asked me over her cup of hot cocoa.

I sighed, flipping through the only magazine in the hospital waiting room. "Yes, I'm sure."

We'd been in the waiting room for two hours. Dad and Gail had been at the hospital for several hours before that. Who knew when the baby was going to come? At first, Destry and I had been pacing nervously. Then we decided to sit. And rehash my horrible night.

"You saw their lips physically touch," Destry said.

"Argh!" I tossed the magazine on a side table. "No! I didn't want to watch it happen, okay? But I know they did." I slumped in the chair. "By Monday, they'll be an official couple."

Destry shook her head. "It doesn't make any sense, especially after the way you told me he danced with you."

"Since when does love make any sense?" I said, frowning.

"Love is the only thing that does make sense, *anjinho*," I heard Dad say. I jumped up and saw him standing there in his hospital scrubs, beaming a tired but glowing smile. Destry and I rushed toward him and he wrapped us both in a hug. "So . . . who wants to meet Sabina, your new baby sister?"

I felt a rush of excitement and joy. Destry and I shrieked wildly, jumping up and down until a nurse came over from the reception desk to shush us.

"Sorry," I said. "It's just . . . we have a sister!"

"We heard," she said, smiling as Dad led us down the hallway toward Gail's room. "We get that a lot around here."

Gail was sitting up in bed when we tiptoed in, looking even more tired than Dad but just as teary with joy. In her arms, she cradled a sleeping baby, all bundled up, her little pink mouth puckered.

Sabina.

"She's so tiny!" Destry cried.

"And amazing," I said, marveling at her delicate features.

Gail shifted over in the bed and motioned for me to sit. "Come say hello, big sis," she whispered, and gently laid the baby in my arms.

I stared down at Sabina's face with its ebony eyelashes and bow-shaped lips, not quite believing she was real. My heart felt full.

"Hi, sis," I said softly, stroking her nose. I rocked her for a few minutes, then planted a kiss on top of her beanie-clad head. "Wait till you see your bedroom. We got it all ready for you."

"Is it *my* turn now?" Destry said, tapping her foot impatiently.

"That's your *other* big sis." I stood up so Destry could sit, then passed Sabina carefully to Destry. "She's the bossy one."

"Hey there," Destry said, but she was grinning, already ogling over Sabina like I had.

Dad came over and slid his arm around my shoulder.

"Hi, honey." He kissed the top of my head. "I haven't told you yet how beautiful you look tonight," he said.

"That's okay." I laughed. "I think there's a good reason for you to be preoccupied."

Dad smiled but his eyes turned teary, and he pulled me into a hug. "I'm so glad you're here with us for this," he said. "There've been so many other times I wish I could've shared with you." He looked at me thoughtfully. "I know you would've probably rather gone with your mom to Switzerland, but—"

"No," I interrupted him, shaking my head. "I don't feel that way. Not anymore." I took a deep breath. "I've actually been thinking that, if it's okay with you, maybe I could stay with you until the end of summer. I could help with Sabina, and maybe we could still catch a few Red Sox games. I mean, if it's not any trouble."

"Trouble?" Dad laughed, giving me a huge hug. "How could you even think that? Your mom and I will need to talk about it, but we'd love to have you with us, for as long as you'd like."

"It would be wonderful," Gail said, smiling while Destry cooed over Sabina.

Worry passed over Dad's face as he glanced back at me. "But . . . are you sure? About staying longer?"

I glanced at Gail and Destry and Sabina, then at my dad's proud face, so full of love. This *was* my family, as much as Mom and Bill were. For the first time, I felt like a true part of it. Not a part being wedged into place out of necessity or circumstance, but a part made to fit.

"I'm sure." I gave Dad a kiss on the cheek, smiling. "This is exactly where I want to be."

Chapter
Fourteen

I had no idea what time it was when Dad finally took Destry and me home from the hospital, but Saturday night had become Sunday morning by the time we fell into bed, exhausted but too excited to sleep.

When I finally drifted off, it seemed as though I'd only closed my eyes for a few seconds when I heard the doorbell ringing. Dad had told us that he was going back to the hospital as soon as the sun came up, so I knew he wouldn't answer the door. And across the room, Destry was snoring like a gurgling teapot, so it was me or nobody.

I stumbled out of bed, eyes still half closed and, after pulling on my sweats, felt my way to the door. I peered through the keyhole, then groaned inwardly at the sight of Viv, holding a stuffed pink unicorn and looking uncharacteristically nervous.

"Open up, Lise," she said, knocking loudly. "I know you're in there. I can practically hear you thinking how much you hate me."

I took a deep breath and opened the door. "I don't hate you," I said grudgingly. "But the unicorn is up for debate."

"Really?" Viv said, giving the unicorn a squeeze, then pushing past me into the house. "Good thing it's for the baby, then." She giggled nervously, but when she saw I wasn't returning her smile, she sighed. "Look, we need to talk."

I folded my arms. "There's nothing to talk about. I saw you kissing Raj last night. I know I have to get over him, and I will. Because . . ." I stared at the ground, and took a deep breath. "Because I don't want to lose your friendship. It's just going to take a little while."

"Wait." Viv's eyes widened. "Kissing?"

I nodded. "Under the gazebo. I saw you when I was leaving the dance."

Viv shook her head. "I don't know what you thought you saw,

but we weren't kissing. Anything but." A frown pulled at her mouth. "I was ending it with him."

I gaped at her. "But why?"

"I saw the way he was looking at you while you were dancing. He's never looked at me like that. But even before that, I knew it wasn't going to work. I just didn't want to admit it."

I bit my lip, confused. "One dance doesn't mean he's into me," I said.

"No, but *this* does." Viv plopped the unicorn into my hands, reached into her messenger bag, and pulled out Raj's sketch-book. "Raj left his sketchbook in my dad's car on the way to the dance last night. Since his mom picked him up right after our talk, I didn't get a chance to give it back to him. I guess he did this sketch after our Concord trip," she said softly. She flipped the sketchbook open to a page in the middle, then held it up for me to see.

I stared at the page as my knees turned to putty. There *I* was, drawn in charcoal and pastels, my face tilted toward an unseen sun, my eyes closed, a daydreamy smile on my lips, my dark hair spilling out behind me and twining with a tangerine breeze that blew across the page.

"It's not me he likes," Viv whispered. "It's you."

"But . . . but . . ." For once, I didn't have words, written or otherwise, to match the moment. A million thoughts raced through my head.

"I was horrible for acting the way I did," Viv continued sadly. "Raj wasn't ever mine to begin with. We're not right for each other. Not even close. But I got caught up in his niceness." She smiled. "And then, well, you know how I get with boys." She gave a shrug. "I wanted to like him, but honestly, I couldn't. Not when I kept feeling guilty. I'm sorry."

"Me too," I said, feeling a jumble of emotions. "It was as much my fault as yours. I should've told Raj the truth about who I was from the very beginning. It wasn't fair of me to put you in that position with him, and then expect it not to get complicated." I glanced at her. "So . . . can we be friends again?"

Viv grinned, then hugged me. "We never weren't." She pulled away, looking at me sternly. "But *you* have to do something to make things right. You have to tell him the truth!"

"I can't," I said. "It's too late. When he finds out I've been lying this whole time, he'll never want to speak to me again."

"Maybe. Or . . . maybe not. There's only one way to find out."

"But what about you?" I asked, biting my lip.

"Don't worry about me," Viv said with a suspiciously cheerful smile.

My mouth dropped open when I saw a blush creeping over her cheeks. "Are you kidding me? Don't tell me you're already onto *another* crush? Who is it?"

I'd never seen her so flustered before, but she finally blurted, "Kyan."

I burst out laughing and clapping. "It's *about* time!"

"I knew you knew he liked me!" Viv declared. "You were dropping hints about him all along, and I was oblivious, right?"

"Pretty much," I said teasingly. "But . . . when?"

"At the dance," Viv said shyly. "Raj left after we talked, and Kyan and I ended up hanging out for hours. We talked about the stuff going on with my mom, and how she was going to let me take a break from modeling. I told him that I was thinking about running for student body later this spring, and he offered to help me with the campaign! Then he asked me to dance out in the gazebo, and then, the next thing I knew, we were kissing! And . . . it was amazing!"

I laughed. "We *are* talking about Kyan?"

She blushed all over again. "I never would have guessed it. But he completely swept me off my feet. He's so kind, and thoughtful, and cute, even with the bug thing."

I laughed. So Kyan had gotten his Casanova on. I couldn't wait to call him later. "Just don't go all praying mantis on him, okay?"

"Me? Never going to happen," Viv said adamantly. "Not with a guy like him."

And here's what was *really* crazy. For once, I believed her.

"Here," Viv said, putting Raj's sketchbook in my hands. "You should be the one to give this back to Raj."

I nodded, my pulse picking up at the mere thought of telling Raj the truth.. "I have no idea how I'm going to do this." But then, suddenly, I *did* know, and it was perfect.

"We have to go," I said, grabbing my coat and pulling her toward the door as I checked my watch. "It's eleven," I mumbled, more to myself than to Viv. "Madame Leroux should be there already, getting ready for the Grand Opening in five hours . . ."

"Wait!" Viv said. "What are you talking about? And who's Madame Leroux?" She stopped in the doorway stubbornly.

"I'll tell you everything while we walk." I scribbled a quick note to Destry and left it propped up against the inside of the door.

"Okay," Viv said hesitantly. "But . . . where are we going?"

"Swoonful of Sugar," I said. "I just figured out how I'm going to tell Raj who I am."

• • • • •

The Grand Opening was scheduled for four p.m. After stopping by the hospital to see Sabina, and then rushing home and changing, I was back outside Swoonful at three forty-five.

I kept pacing outside the door. I tried my best to look nonchalant, but since pacing is anything but, it only took a few minutes for Madame Leroux to take pity on me.

"*Bienvenue, cherie*," she said, waving me into the patisserie. Even with her apron on, she looked elegant, with her hair in a perfect chignon. "You've come to check up on my decorating skills, yes?"

"Oh no," I blustered. "I mean, I just wanted to see . . ." My voice trailed off in embarrassment.

Her laugh had soothing bell tones. She turned toward the long wall behind the café tables, sweeping an arm in the air with a grand gesture. "Now tell me. Does the display meet your approval? I think it has that certain *je ne sais quoi*, don't you?"

I glanced at the twelve paintings and sketches hanging carefully along the wall. I'd chosen them earlier today after asking Madame Leroux if she needed some inspiring artwork to go along with her delicious pastries. I'd chosen my favorite pieces from Raj's sketchbook, and they looked brilliant on the wall, their vivacious strokes and bright colors fitting in perfectly with the atmosphere, like this was where they belonged.

"I love it," I said. "I hope he does, too."

Madame Leroux nodded as she slid her apron from over her head, tucking it behind the counter. "What you've done, you've done from the heart. He will see that."

"*If* he comes," I said.

It was a big *if*, and as the minutes passed and four o'clock came and went, I started to think that he wouldn't. Madame Leroux was handing out free macarons, and customers streamed in steadily. She put a brimming plateful of them in front of me, too, but my stomach was too full of butterflies to eat any. Soon, nearly every table was full, except for the one I was sitting at, which had the clearest view of the front door.

Then, at last, I saw him. He came in wearing the same sweater he'd had on the night we first met, and his expression, one of hopeful nervousness, made me smile. Just as I was wondering how long it would take him to notice, his eyes flitted to the art on the walls, and his mouth fell open. I took a deep breath, taking that as my cue, and walked toward him with a racing heart.

"Do you like it?" I asked softly.

He started at the sound of my voice, then smiled. "Hey, Lise," he said. "So you decided to do the review today after all?"

"Um . . . maybe," I said cryptically. "But that's not the real reason I'm here."

"Oh," he said distractedly. "Did you come with Viv? Where is she?" He waved at his paintings, blushing. "I . . . I can't believe she did this. It's amazing."

My pulse roared in my ears. *Tell him, tell him, tell him.* "Viv didn't do it," I blurted. "I did."

"You?" he repeated, shaking his head in confusion. "But I got an email from her this afternoon, saying she was sorry she hadn't been telling the truth. She said to meet her here, and she'd explain everything."

"Was it from the Frog Princess?" I asked weakly, even though I knew the answer. When he nodded, I gathered up every ounce of my courage and confessed. "That's me. I'm the Frog Princess."

"What?" he breathed, staring.

I nodded. "I was the girl you met here on Valentine's Day." My face was on fire, and I couldn't breathe. But I had to keep going. I had to tell the whole truth. "I didn't know who you were, or how to find you. By the time I finally figured out who you were . . ." I swallowed. This was the tough part. "I was too chicken to tell you who *I* was. And you were so different in the pressroom, bossing everyone around, that I wasn't sure—"

"That you liked me," he finished for me as a shadow crossed his face. "So you and Viv switched places." He frowned.

"It was wrong. And I'm sorry I lied to you."

"I can't believe this." The disappointment in his eyes made my stomach churn. "You and Viv . . ." He shook his head. "Was it like a game to you?"

"No!" I cried. "It wasn't like that at all. I only asked her to pretend to be me so that I could get to know you, and then things spiraled out of control. It was so stupid of me. All because I was too stubborn to admit how much . . ." My voice shook.

"How much I really like you, and have from the very beginning." *Oh my god.* Had I actually admitted that to him out loud?

Raj stared at the ground for what seemed like an eternity, and I waited for his expression to lighten, but it didn't. Finally, he lifted his eyes to mine. "A part of me knew something was wrong," he said quietly. "Something with Viv felt off from the beginning. But I kept remembering how Valentine's Day was, and hoping the connection would come back. And you started working on the paper, and I got to know you, and then . . ." My heart lifted with hope as he paused. But he only sighed heavily. "How can I trust you after everything that's happened? I don't know who you really are."

Pain stabbed my heart, and I felt the hopes I'd had crumbling. "Yes, you do," I protested. "I'm the same girl you met here on Valentine's Day. Every time I talked to you as the princess, or in the pressroom. That was me. All of it. You have to believe that."

His eyes were doubtful and sad. "What if . . . I can't?" He turned toward the door.

"Wait!" I blurted, then hurried back to my table for my bag. "I have something for you." I pulled out his sketchbook, and then the watercolor he'd done of Boston Harbor that he'd given me on Valentine's Day. "I love this so much, but . . . I don't deserve it. Not after what I did. I should've given it back to you forever ago, but I guess I had a hard time letting it go."

Raj took his sketchbook, but shook his head at the watercolor. "I want you to keep it."

I nodded, not able to speak through my terrible dread that this was his version of good-bye.

He glanced toward the door. "I—I think I know what I need to do now, but I really have to go—"

"Raj, wait! I wanted to say . . ." I sighed, then whispered, "I hope we can still be friends."

He nodded thoughtfully. "I'm not sure that's possible, Lise." Then he was gone.

I stared at the closing door with filling eyes, feeling as if my fate had been sealed. Madame Leroux came over, her face deepening with worry.

"*Mon dieu* . . . where did he go?" she said. "He can't walk away from what was meant to be!"

A single tear slid down my cheek. "He just did." And then, grabbing my bag and leaving my plate of untouched macarons on the table, so did I.

It was hours before I could stop crying. Destry brought me some chocolate, but she was helpless to stop the flood. Finally, she tucked a box of tissues beside me in bed, and I fell asleep clutching a wad of them, my pillow damp, my heart aching.

I was dreaming of a smiling Madame Leroux when a sound like rain woke me. I lifted my head from the pillow, listening in the dark. There it was again. Tiny, scattered tappings on the windowpane. But it wasn't rain. It was . . . pebbles?

"Destry," I whispered into the moonlit room. "Do you hear that?"

"Mmmmph" came the answer, followed by a groan. "This better be good," she whined, just as another *ping!* sounded on the glass. She yanked up her eye mask and lifted the blind, peering outside. "Great," she mumbled. "Some crazy stalker with a plateful of tiny pink burgers."

Tiny pink burgers . . .

"What?" I shrieked, leaping out of my bed and pouncing on hers, making her holler in protest. Outside on the lawn was Raj, peering up at the window, a plateful of macarons in his hands.

"Omigod," I hissed. "It's *him*!"

"No kidding," Destry deadpanned, yawning. "He *had* to show up at midnight, didn't he? He couldn't wait for morning like a normal human being." But even as she said it, she was grinning.

"What do I do?" I asked.

"Are you kidding?" She gave me a playful shove. "Get out of your self-pity slump and get down there!"

I laughed and gave her a hug. "You know, I think I might learn to like sharing a room with you."

"Yeah, yeah." She waved me away. "Now . . . go!"

Trying to tiptoe *and* run at the same time, I managed to make it downstairs and outside in record time, slipping into my boots and coat on the way. The lawn was tinged blue with moonlight. Seeing Raj smile made my heart soar.

"Hey there, Princess," he said softly. "Would you like a macaron? The two halves connect two people, or so I've been told."

"I—I—what are you doing here?" I stuttered. "I thought you hated me. When you left Swoonful, you said we'd never be friends."

"Because we can't be, when we're already more."

Oh. My heart swelled. *Oh!*

"But . . . then why did you leave?" I pressed, still trying to make sense of everything.

"I left to go find my dad." His smile widened. "I convinced him to come back to the patisserie with me, so that I could show him my art. He actually, unbelievably, liked it! And he agreed to let me take art classes in high school next year, as long as I keep up my grades."

"That's great, Raj," I said, smiling. "I'm really happy for you."

He stepped closer, peering at me intently with those blooming desert eyes. "It's because of you," he whispered, gently brushing a strand of hair from my face. His hand moved from my face to my waist, and stayed there. "You know, these last few weeks, I wasn't being honest, either. There's something I haven't told you yet."

"What?" I said, electrified by the warmth of his hand.

"Part of me believed you were her all along. I almost asked you a couple times, but never went through with it." He leaned closer. "I wanted *you* to be the princess. Even from the start."

I felt dizzy with surprise and joy. "You did?"

He nodded and took my face between his hands. "You're perfect for me, Lise. I think we were both too stubborn to realize it.

But that's why I did that drawing of you at Author's Ridge that day. You inspire me. You looked so beautiful, sitting there daydreaming." He paused, bringing his face closer to mine. "You *are* so beautiful."

I grinned at him as my heart raced. "You're not so bad yourself."

Raj smiled. "So . . . tell me one more time. How does the frog turn back into a princess?"

I smiled up at him, barely able to breathe. "A kiss?"

"Don't mind if I do," he said.

His lips met mine, soft and lingering. As I fell under their spell, I remembered my dream of Madame Leroux, and I wondered if somewhere, somehow, she was smiling right now. The Frog Princess had finally found her prince, and without Swoonful of Sugar, it would never have happened.

I smiled, knowing exactly what I'd write in its review come Monday morning:

One thing about Swoonful of Sugar is certain. The macarons are as sweet as a crush, and as magical as a midnight, moonlit kiss.

Macarons Recipes

In the mood for some macarons at midnight? Lise and Raj enjoyed these scrumptious treats, and now you can try making your own! Just remember to always use adult supervision when you're using a stove top or oven, or when you're handling hot foods. And, most importantly, enjoy these sweets with all the sweethearts in your life!

Vanilla Cream Macarons

For the macarons:

> 1 cup powdered sugar
> ½ cup almond meal
> 2 egg whites (at room temperature)
> 4 tbsp granulated sugar
> 1 pastry bag with plain tip
> ½ tsp vanilla extract
> ½ cup vanilla buttercream frosting (can be found in local supermarket)

Preheat oven to 350° Fahrenheit. Line two baking sheets with wax paper. In a blender or food processor, mix powdered sugar and almond meal until it becomes a fine powder. With a hand-held mixer, beat the egg whites in a small bowl until they begin to stiffen. Slowly add in the granulated sugar until the mixture is fluffy and forms little peaks (about 1–2 minutes). Add the vanilla extract until it is blended evenly. Slowly and gently fold the dry mixture into the whipped egg whites, stirring with a spatula until well-blended. Spoon the batter into the pastry bag. Squeeze the batter into 1-inch circles onto the baking sheets, spacing them about an inch apart. Tap the baking sheet on the counter until the circles flatten slightly on the sheet. Bake for approximately 15–18 minutes. Remove from the oven and let cool completely before removing from the baking sheet. Spread a spoonful of vanilla buttercream filling gently onto the flat side of one of the wafers. Then sandwich two of the wafers together. Wait one day before serving to let the flavors blend together. *Bon appetit!*

Chocolate Macarons with Ganache Filling

For the macarons:

- 1 cup powdered sugar
- ½ cup almond meal
- 4 tbsp unsweetened cocoa powder
- 2 egg whites (at room temperature)
- 4 tbsp granulated sugar
- 1 pastry bag with plain tip

Preheat oven to 350° Fahrenheit. Line two baking sheets with wax paper. In a blender or food processor, mix powdered sugar, almond meal, and cocoa until it becomes a fine powder. With a hand-held mixer, beat the egg whites in a small bowl until they begin to stiffen. Slowly add in the granulated sugar until the mixture is fluffy and forms little peaks (about 1–2 minutes). Slowly and gently fold the dry chocolate mixture into the whipped egg whites, stirring with a spatula until well-blended. Spoon the batter into the pastry bag. Squeeze the batter into 1-inch circles onto the baking sheets, spacing them about an inch apart. Tap the baking sheet on the counter until the circles flatten slightly on the sheet. Bake for approximately 15–18 minutes. Remove from the oven and let cool completely before removing from the baking sheet. Make your ganache filling.

Once the ganache filling has cooled completely, spread it gently onto the flat side of one of the chocolate wafers. Then sandwich two of the wafers together. Wait one day before serving to let the flavors blend together. *Bon appetit!*

For the ganache filling:

  ½ cup heavy cream
  4 oz. chopped semi-sweet baking chocolate

Put chopped chocolate into a medium bowl. Boil cream in a sauce-pan. Pour the cream over the chocolate and mix until well-blended.

Raspberry Macarons with Raspberry Jam Filling

For the macarons:

- 1 cup powdered sugar
- ½ cup almond meal
- 2–3 drops red food coloring
- 2 egg whites (at room temperature)
- 4 tbsp granulated sugar
- 1 pastry bag with plain tip
- ½ cup seedless raspberry jam

Preheat oven to 350° Fahrenheit. Line two baking sheets with wax paper. In a blender or food processor, mix powdered sugar and almond meal until it becomes a fine powder. With a hand-held mixer, beat the egg whites in a small bowl until they begin to stiffen. Slowly add in the granulated sugar until the mixture is fluffy and forms little peaks (about 1–2 minutes). Add the food coloring and stir until the red is blended evenly. Slowly and gently fold the dry mixture into the whipped egg whites, stirring with a spatula until well-blended. Spoon the batter into the pastry bag. Squeeze the batter into 1-inch circles onto the baking sheets, spacing them about an inch apart. Tap the baking sheet on the counter until the circles flatten slightly on the sheet. Bake for approximately 15–18 minutes. Remove from the oven and let cool completely before removing from the baking sheet. Spread a spoonful of raspberry jam gently onto the flat side of one of the pink wafers. Then sandwich two of the wafers together. Wait one day before serving to let the flavors blend together. *Bon appetit!*

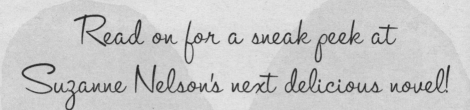

Read on for a sneak peek at
Suzanne Nelson's next delicious novel!

Alex held a cup out to me. "Here. Try some. You look like you could use it."

"Thanks," I said, waving the cup away, "but I don't like hot chocolate."

"Who ever heard of an elf that doesn't like hot chocolate?" He laughed. "Isn't that against the big guy's rules?" There was a teasing glimmer in his eyes.

"It's not my thing. Too sweet and syrupy. Ick." I shook my head, grimacing.

His eyes widened. "Man, if you've got something against hot chocolate, you must be having one *bad* day."

"*Bad* is an understatement." We stepped back as Mom moved in with her camera to snap the photos of Tommy with Dad. I popped a piece of my favorite hard candy, Venom, into my mouth. The tart watermelon and spicy pepper flavors zinged over my taste buds, cheering me up a bit. Then, while Alex handed out the rest of the hot chocolates, I recounted every detail of my traumatic morning to him. It felt so good to unload all of my frustrations, even onto a stranger. "I've been bitten, stomped on, and yelled at," I finished in summary, "and if I hear one more Christmas song, I'll scream." I sighed. "I hate the holiday season."

Alex laughed. "You hate Christmas? I love this time of year!"

"Somehow, that doesn't surprise me." I motioned to his sweater.

"Hey, if you can't wear an ugly sweater at Christmastime, when can you? Besides, it's my work uniform. Abuelo has Frosty the Snowman on his."

I couldn't help grinning at that.

"So, what's your problem with Christmas?" He leaned closer, whispering, "Wait, don't tell me. Your grandpa got run over by a reindeer?"

I laughed. It was impossible not to. He was funny, I had to give him that. "Christmas," I said, "is a completely commercialized holiday that feeds on materialism. It's just another way for stores to make money off customers who feel obligated to buy meaningless gifts for people they probably don't even like."

"Whoa." Alex shook his head, holding up a hand for mercy. "I wonder if they offer elf training workshops in anger management."

I wanted to look mad, but another laugh broke through instead.

"Seriously, though," he said, his eyes holding mine. "It's too bad you feel that way. Christmas is the season of love and giving . . ."

As if on cue, a child's voice rose up from the line, whining, "But *why* won't you buy me that doll, Mommy? It's only thirty dollars, and you said I could have a treat today!"

I jerked my thumb in the direction of the voice. "See? Nothing but 'gimme gimme.'"

Alex only smiled. "You can't blame an overtired kid for trying." He shrugged. "And if you're hoping to convert me, it's not going to work."

I raised a skeptical eyebrow at him. "There's no way you can stay legitimately happy through all of this."

"So what are you saying? That I'm faking it?" He studied me in a thoughtful way that made me fidget self-consciously with my costume. It was like his eyes were searching for something inside of me I didn't even know was there. It was unsettling, *and* irritating.

"Yeah," I admitted. "Maybe you are."

"Or . . ." He leaned toward me, jingling the bell on my hat, and warmth flooded through me. I felt momentarily disoriented at his closeness. "Maybe you're wrong. And maybe *I* can change your mind. Starting with hot chocolate."

I snorted, the spell broken. "I don't change my mind about much. Just ask my parents."

"Then you're in even worse shape than I thought." He shook his head at me, then looked past me toward Cocoa Cravings, where his *abuelo* was motioning him over. "I've got to get back to the shop." He picked up his empty tray. "But since we're going to be working next door to each other, I'm sure I'll see you again. Better watch out. Optimism can be contagious, you know."

I rolled my eyes. "I'm immune."

He turned to walk away, but as he did, a small penguin waddled in front of him, followed by two puffing, out-of-shape security guards.

"Come back here, Happy Feet!" one of them hollered.

Alex and I looked at each other, then burst out laughing.

He started walking again, calling over his shoulder, "See you around, Scrooge!"

I stared after him, surprised by how much I had laughed today.

"Break time's over," Mom said, tapping me on the shoulder. "I need you to help set up the next shot." When I hesitated, Mom handed me a basket of candy canes. "Well, come on, Em! Get over there and spread some cheer."

I sighed. This was going to be the longest holiday season of my life.

Find more reads you will love . . .

Rory Swenson has been waiting her whole life to turn twelve. And she's got a list to prove it. Whenever Rory asks her parents for something, they always say, "When you're twelve . . ." Well, in exactly 18 hours, 36 minutes, and 52 seconds it will finally happen. Rory's life will officially begin!

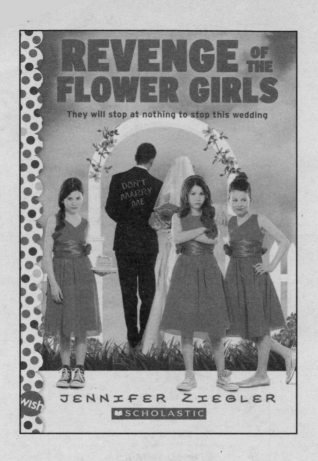

The Brewster triplets—Dawn, Darby, and Delaney—
are stuck helping their big sister, Lily, plan her
wedding. Burton, Lily's groom-to-be, is not nice or
fun, and he looks like an armadillo. The flower girls
will stop at nothing to delay Lily's big day, but will
sprinklers, a photo slideshow, a muddy dog, and some
unexpected allies be enough to prevent their big sister
from living unhappily ever after?

Kara McAllister just had her best idea yet. She's going to take notes on all of the boys she knows in order to answer a seemingly simple question: How can she get a boyfriend? But Kara's project turns out to be a lot more complicated than she imagined. Soon there are secrets, lies, and an embarrassing incident in the boys' bathroom. Still, if Kara's research leads her to the right boy, everything may just be worth it . . .

How to spot a  book

EYE-CATCHING SPINES!

FUN & FRIENDSHIP INSIDE!

IRRESISTIBLE STORIES!

PLUS, FIRST CRUSHES!

■ SCHOLASTIC

scholastic.com

SCHOLASTIC and associated logos are trademarks and/or registered trademarks of Scholastic Inc.

WISH1